Chronicles of Crumb

Conversations with my Pointy Nosed Counter Surfing Bastard Hound

Nicola Marie Jackson

Caveat, or a warning (something that a barrister friend said I should add)

These are the very off-the-wall jottings of the slave of a very special whippet (or Pointy-Nosed Counter Surfing Bastard Hound) called Crumb. They were originally published in a slightly amended form on various Facebook Group pages including on 'Mad About Whippets.'

If you are a dog lover, particularly a whippet fancier, you will understand some of the nuances and mannerisms of my dear Crumb. If you hate dogs, this book is probably not for you. If you received it as a present and you fall into this category, may I suggest that you pass it on to someone who may appreciate the humour and irony expressed in this volume.

If you are of nervous disposition, easily offended by bad language, irreligious ideation or by irreverent references to television personalities, move down the shop and look under Barbara Cartland or Enid Blyton.

If you are able to read joined-up writing and a dog lover, you will just love this book. Well I hope that you do! Ask an adult to buy it for you and don't be caught reading it. Your parents may not approve (rude bits)! If you're 'of a certain age' or prone to 'leaks' make sure you're near a toilet as you could pee yourself laughing.

Author's special notes:

Fifteen percent of the net sale of this book will be donated to dog charities of the Author's choice.

If you would like your very own personalised copy of Chronicles of Crumb, pawtographed by Crumbolina herself, all you need to do is to send me an email requesting a copy to nicolamj75@gmail.com. I will respond with the address and instructions. Then send me a copy of the printed book, with a self-addressed prepaid envelope, mentioning any particular message or dedication that you would like added and including either a cheque for £5.00 or a copy of your PayPal receipt for that amount sent to my email address with your name and town as the reference. The money will be used as a donation to Whippet Rescue UK or the Dog's Trust or some other worthy animal cause. If you prefer to make a donation of some dog food to a doggie charity, please send details with your book.

Dedication

This book is dedicated to my wonderful Dad who encouraged my reading by shouting "Did you get Nicola a book?" when my mum would drag home dozens of bags of gifts through the door. That was his sole contribution to his kids' Christmas gifts. My lovely mum was so patient with that man. So very, very patient. I believe I get my sense of humour from him as none of my family will take the blame. When I went to see him in hospital he was laughing because he had convinced a few of his mates that the doctors were so impressed the size of his manhood that they were writing an article about it for The Lancet. He told them that certain nurses had begged, that's right begged, to see his penis because they couldn't believe the rumours. Dad, generous as always, always gave them a flash and all were so impressed but we're sad as he had ruined them for other men. My sister spoke about this as my Dad's funeral home in what I believe was a first for the Crematorium and I think that says all you need to know about my family. God I miss you my Pa.

Acknowledgments

Personally, the only person I think that I should thank is me, because I wrote the book, but my friends and family think of it, the book, as a child and they are the village that helps raise them, so here we go:

I would like to thank my Mum and my sisters Alix and Casey. Casey is the only one who reads my writing as Mum and Alix's Mum say that I confuse them. Alix says I fry her brain. Thank you, Casey for looking after my four-pawed wet-nosed cretin. I appreciate it oodles and I'm sorry she poos on your bed.

I would also like to thank Auntie Toffee Penny for loving Crumb and for all the gifts you have bought her and the support you have given us, we both think you're fab! Thank you to Carrie and Jo, *aka* Team Crumb, for being there for us and everyone in Mad About Whippets, who have shown Fruitcake (me) and Crumb lots of love.

But the reason you are holding this book is because of Crumb's Godparents, Marion and Robert, who we call Budma and Budpa (he's a Buddhist so that's why it's Budma and Budpa). This wonderful couple has turned my Crumbversations (conversations with Crumb) into a book and this has involved a lot of proof-reading, which can't have been easy, as quite often I'll type a word and spell check is like 'What is this? What the Hell do you expect me to do with 8 vowels and 3 consonants, do I look like a frigging magician?' But more importantly, they have been there for me during every 'I can't fucking write!' moment and made me believe that I CAN write. I just can't spell, and grammar is something that schools used to be.

Having you lot in my corner is wonderful.

Thank you, all of you.

Nicola, xxx

Introduction

Chronicles of Crumb started on Mad About Whippets, a Facebook group for people who have a fondness for the small slim dogs who look like they own iPhones and run a travel blog. Crumb came into my life as my sister said I could have one of her dog's pups when she gave birth on 17th September 2015. There were nine pups and I said I would have whatever pup was left after her friends and family had had their pick.

I found out that everyone wanted Titch as she was tiny, while no-one who was offered Crumb wanted her as she was the biggest and had one white side while others had all over markings. I was thinking about her and realised that she's a big girl, doesn't make the best first impression and has smaller, prettier sisters, and then it hit me, she's a furry me! And that's when I knew she was mine.

My sister had called her Chummy but I called her Crumb as my nieces and nephews call me Fruitcake, and she's Crumb, as she's a piece of me. I started uploading our chats (or Crumbversations as they soon became known) on Facebook purely as I wanted to get more likes on a post than my sister, but I carried on because I discovered the pointy-nosed little sod was far more popular than I ever was. Crumb has told me several times that dogs don't talk, but she also told me that it wasn't her on Motorway Cops on Channel 5 being chased down the M1, but it clearly is her so I can't trust what's she's saying. As you can understand, that's a conundrum ...

I hope you enjoy reading this, but if you don't, can I still keep the money? I need to have a lawyer on retainer due to Crumb's antics, and infuriatingly, they don't do any Groupon deals.

What Facebook readers have said about Crumbversations

"It made me belly laugh. Thank you Crumb is too clever!" – B.C.

"Great start for going to work at ridiculous hours – C.S.

"I laughed so hard at this!" – G.H.

"Would love to have seen a picture of the glitter poo. Very creative whippet girl." – N.S.

"Fan-bloody-tastic!!" – W.C.C.

"Utterly completely brilliant!!!" – N.H.

"What a hoot!" – J.W.

"Oh Crumb and Fruitcake this is hilarious, I never ever laughed so much in my life while reading your chronicles, they say laughter is the best medicine, you've certainly cured me." - L.R.

"Managed to not splurt the coffee - just !" - A.F.

"First class. Absolutely brilliant. Can't wait for the next instalment" – L.E.

"I'm on a streetcar on way to work reading this and everyone is staring as I'm crying with laughter. You both are hysterical…" - D.H.

"Hoomon vocab doesn't contain enough words of the correct quality to describe how superb this is." – J.W.

"Laughed myself incontinent!" – R.W.T.

Editors' Note

We weren't sure whether to call this an Editors' Note or a Translator's Comment. Until we met the lovely Nicola, and were introduced to her charming writing, we knew about some regional variations in the English dialect, such as Cockney, Scouse and Geordie. We even recognised a Welsh lilt and the Scottish brogue. Then we learned that there was another previously hidden dialect, complete with its own vocabulary and colloquialisms. Ilkeston has its own language. Not a lot of people know that. Slowly we began to lean to its charming idiosyncratic additions to the English language, additions not limited to references to body parts or functions but extending also to everyday greetings and insults.

We make no apology for refusing to edit out these.

Stay away Your Highness

Crumb has the bag on and she's grumpy because we went for a long walk and I refused to carry her when she was tired.

Crumb: *Sits up faster than a coked-up rattlesnake*

I am a delicate and oh-so-fragile waif and I refuse to be dragged around Ilkeston like a common cur!

Me: I'm sorry Crumb but you are not a featherweight dog and …

Crumb: Are you fat shaming me?

Me: Of course not Crumb, but I can't carry…

Crumb: You are! You're fat shaming me!

Me: Crumb, calm down, all I was saying is that I just can't carry you for the 2 hours we were out.

Crumb: I never asked you to carry me! I gave you multiple options you grape ape!

Me: I can't ... grape ape? Was that because I've died my hair purple?

Crumb: No, it's my way of protesting the high cost of housing in London, OF COURSE IT'S FOR YOUR HAIR, YOU GRADE A LISTED TIT!

Me: You're grounded.

Crumb: I can't go out anyway, I no longer have the long sleek legs that I'm world renowned for!

Me: Oh, dear Jesus and his heavenly elves quit moaning.

Crumb: When I left here this morning, I had legs so curvy and beautiful that Naomi Campbell has been threatening to have me shot!

Me: No, she didn't.

Crumb: Are you calling me a liar?

Me: Yes. Yes, I am.

Crumb: So, you've broken my body and now you're slandering my name!

Me: Your body is fine.

Crumb: Have you no eyes?! I don't have my elegant whippet legs anymore - I have stubs!

Me: It's like living with the residents of Eastenders having you in my life.

Crumb: Are you not bothered that your life choices have left me looking like a loaf with a head?

Me: Your. Legs. Are. Fine.

Crumb: When I went for a wee, the Queen saw me and tried to steal me because I look like a frigging corgi! And I didn't ask you to carry me, although I weigh less than one of your arse cheeks, so it shouldn't have been a problem.

Me: Are you fat shaming me?

Crumb: Yes, but only because you are fat.

Me: You are a pure joy today.

Crumb: Oh I'm so sorry, is my disability bothering you?

Pretends to wipe a tear from her eye

I feel so bad for you.

Me: Crumb. You wanted me to knock a pensioner off his mobility scooter and steal it.

Crumb: I was only thinking of you.

Me: Me? How does your robbing an old person help me?

Crumb: Well, I reasoned, for I have been blessed with rare intellect.

Me: Well I'm with you 100% on that.

Crumb: I'm going to look at that sentence later on in greater detail, but yes, I was thinking of you. If you robbed an able-bodied person, they would have chased you, but if you rob someone who can't walk, then you could hop away on a pogo stick and it matters not, they ain't gonna catch you.

Me: OK, that's actually quite clever.

Crumb: That's 'cus of my massive amount of grey matter up here

Pats her head.

Anyhoo, we can try it if you want, see if it works in practise.

Me: No.

Crumb: Oh, come on, we can bond over a healthy outdoor activity. Let's go whack that arse at No. 31. He called me a thief.

Me: Why?

Crumb: 'Cus I stole from him. Sometimes you really don't think, do you?

Me: We aren't going to assault an old person.

Crumb: He's only 40, go get your shoes on.

Me: No.

Crumb: Oh, come on! I'll even let you swing me like a club, let's knock that motherfucker into 2025!

Me: No.

Crumb: You're such a pussy!

Slinks off upstairs while giving me dirty looks

Later, about 10pm, I hear her come in.

Me: You OK Crumb?

Crumb: I'm feeling a little bit sad.

Me: Oh sweetie, can I do anything for you?

Crumb: No, you will say no if I ask you?

Me: I won't, what can I do?

Crumb: *Sighs*

It doesn't matter.

Me: I promise if it's in my power, I will do it.

Crumb: *Looks hopeful*

Promise?

Me: I promise.

Crumb: I love you!

Me: I love you too Crumb.

Crumb: *Runs outside*

Back in a sec!

Me: What did you want?

Crumb: An alibi. Onward my noble steed!

Rides in on a mobility scooter

Me: I just don't learn.

Rapper Crumb

Crumb: I have a couple of important announcements to make. Yo!

Me: Oh dear God, what have you eaten, destroyed or shat on?

Crumb: I'll ignore that slur on my character for the time being but please don't think I have forgotten because I haven't. Anyway, I have something important to share. Yo!

Me: Why do you keep saying 'Yo!'? And have you purloined Peter's hoodie? You have haven't you, you've nicked his hoodie?

Crumb: They are part of my news: I want to be a rapper and from now on I will only answer to my street name, Crumb Dog Millionaire. Yo!

Me: You've just watched 8 Mile, haven't you?

Crumb: Not necessarily. Yo!

Me: Why do you want to be a rapper, Crumb? Crumb? Crumb! Goddamit, why do you want to be a rapper, Crumb Dog Millionaire?

CDM: I've always felt this way, ever since growing up on the mean streets of Detroit and rap is the only way I've felt comfortable expressing myself. Yo!

Me: You're banned from Netflix.

CDM: Oh my God why? Yo!

Me: Really? You have no idea?

CDM: No.

Me: Fine. What happened when you watched E.T?

CDM: I'm drawing a blank. Yo!

Me: You wrapped your little sister in a blanket, put her in a bike basket and road off the roof and crash landed on next doors car. The only reason that we didn't have to pay for the damage is that when Direct Line received his claim form stating the damage was caused by 'Joyriding Whippets' they sent a copy to his doctor and he spent six weeks in a mental health facility.

CDM: Then why don't I remember? Yo!

Me: Concussion. Before I continue, will you stop saying 'Yo!' if I give you a treat?

CDM: Can I have the whole bag?

Me: No.

CDM: Then Yo!

Me: *Prays for strength*

Then after watching Titanic you flooded the bathroom then tried to shove your sister off the raft you made from the chopping block.

CDM: But she was Jack! But she kept biting when I tried to get her to sink but that not my fault, Blame James Cameron, not me! Yo!

Me: Was it James Cameron who filled the bathroom with stuff stolen from next door?

CDM: But the Titanic was a luxurious ocean liner, we couldn't use YOUR stuff as it would have been less Titanic and more Grapes of Wrath. Yo!

Me: Breaking Bad?

CDM: We never actually produced Meth. Yo!

Me: Only because the pharmacist is my friend and she called me to tell me, and I quote 'That idiot whippet of yours is at the counter with a stick-on moustache trying to buy 50 packs of Sudafed'

CDM: Harsh. But I'll get bored with no telly! Yo!

Me: Then go and read, we have many books.

CDM: Fine, but this isn't over.

Me: What are you doing?

CDM: I'm indicating, by pointing to your eyes and then mine, that I am watching you.

Me: It looks like your paw is watching a game of tennis on a panoramic T.V. Go on, bugger off and read, you're doing my head in!

15 minutes later

CDM: 3 questions, firstly isn't everything 50 shades of grey, secondly what's a butt plug and lastly, do I need to put one on my Christmas list?

Me: Sweet Jesus.

A Name for my Fans

Crumb was pondering her online success ... so many likes on Facebook ...

Crumb: I wish to make an announcement.

Drum roll

I have decided to call my fans something. Yes, a group name so while out, say at a fan club, they can introduce themselves as such. Can you guess what I'm going to call them? You'll never guess what, it's very clever!

Me: Deluded? Gullible? Residents of Insaneville?

Crumb: You're just jealous and it's completely understandable. Unknown, unremarkable pleb people often drown in the green lake of envy.

Me: I'm regretting not getting a parrot.

Crumb: True, but could a seed-eater do this?

Tries a high kick and falls over

Me: No, but that just adds to the appeal of having one. Why do you want your fans to have a special name?

Crumb: Why not? It's just what us celebs do. Justin Bieber has Beliebers, One Direction has Directioners, Trump has Twats, it's just how it works. I want all fellow Crumb lovers to have a good strong name so while out they can all be under my clever pointy-nosed name umbrella.

Me: You constantly change your name; you were Crumb Dog Millionaire not that long ago.

Crumb: That's 'cus I'm a whippet who's living in life's fast lane and when you're speeding like The Crumb, then things can change like THAT!

Attempts to click her paws, realises she has no thumbs to go with no fingers and so gives me a dirty look because it's my fault that she can't snap her paws

Soon it could be Dame Crumb if the people who dish out the Honours will just stop being such pussies, cancel the restraining order and read my submission. I believe I make some excellent points on why throwing a Dameship my way would help them.

Me: But all you wrote was 'Make Me A Dame or Spend Every Morning of Your Lifetime De-shitting Your Shoes. How long your particular lifetime lasts is directly correlated to your reply. Please don't try this whippet, I'm fucking relentless.'

Crumb: I know, right? Hardly a restraining order offence!

Me: You sent it 387 times.

Crumb: I was concerned when they didn't reply, I wanted to make sure they received it.

Me: Crumb, you broke into the head of the committee's house and stapled a copy to his head and then you put a copy in every single one of his shoes along with a note saying 'Like finding surprises in your shoes? No? Then Dame the Crumb!'

Crumb: Got him to reply didn't it?

Me: It got the police to reply, Crumb, the POLICE.

Crumb: Same thing.

Me: No, it is not. Anyhoo, you already refer to us as Chimps, whippet.

Crumb: I don't mean normal humans. I'm speaking of those who are "My" people.

Me: YOUR people?

Crumb: Yes, MY people. My fans, followers, those kind people who bathe my soft fur in adoration and who would hurl themselves into a puddle so I could use them as a bridge in order to keep my dainty paws dry. I speak of those generous souls who would defend my good name.

Me: A couple of ants with a noodle sword could do that.

Me: *Throws a shoe at my head. Shoe is not empty. After having a shower and wet-wiping the floor, I return.*

You're grounded.

Crumb: Not a good idea, I have an army of fans who would retaliate on my behalf and you would go down faster than a porn star blowing Trump. It's fast because they want to go and bathe in Listerine in case fascism can be caught like herpes of which I'm sure he has no knowledge off. Just like his creepy sons have no awareness that they seem to drip oil ...

Me: Still grounded.

Crumb: We will see ...

Me: Can you get on with it? I need a wee. Are you going to enlighten me?

Crumb: Yes, but it's such a smart name I can't just blurt it out. I need to explain my thought process. So, I care for my fans like you Chimps, care for your pets.

Me: You're calling your fan base your 'Pets?'

Crumb: Let the whippet finish, woman! I mean it in a nice way. So then, Pets, yes?

Me: Yep.

Crumb: Then I add my moniker into the mix and then I have a name for my homies that's so clever that you will never guess it in a million years. You see, your little chimp brain is used to nothing more taxing than finding the location of your next amusingly shaped fruit. Whereas the whippet you see in front of you is like a furry Shakespeare, my words are the tools I use to …

Me: Crumpets!

Crumb: You what?

Me: You've named them Crumpets, as in Crum(b)pets.

Crumb: What?

Me: Crumpets. I'm right, aren't I?

Crumb: Yes. Well done

Stands up and goes to walk out but at the last moment turns around and smiles at me

Right then, I'm off. I hope you didn't splash your shoes.

Me: What? When did I splash my shoes?

Crumb: WHEN YOU PISSED ON MY CORNFLAKES, YOU COLOSSAL WAXED MAMMOTH'S BALL SACK!

Next door's pet mice

Me: Crumb, may I have a quick word?

Crumb: I don't see why not.

Me: Have you been trying to eat next door's pet mice?

Crumb: And now I see why not

Gets up to flounce off but I grab her collar

Unhand me, you low born tree-swinger and cease your baseless accusations!

Me: He said that you broke in and tried to eat his mice.

Crumb: How dare he! He'd better have some strong evidence if he is going to come here and slur my good name! Does he have any evidence?

Me: Not much.

Crumb: Then how dare he!

Me: Just a photo of you in his kitchen next to the mouse cage with your mouth open and a sign pointing to your mouth saying International House of Cheese. Mice eat free, it's not a trap. Trust the Crumb.

Crumb: Well I'm as shocked as you to hear that. I must have done it while suffering from a high temperature.

People do strange things while ill, my great uncle thought he was Carmen Miranda when he had the flu.

Me: No, he didn't.

Crumb: Paw to God. Carmen Miranda. Although to be fair he realised by all the compliments that he was one of the few whippets who can carry off wearing a small selection of fruit on their head so every cloud and all. Wore a pineapple on his bonce for the rest of his life. Inspired Lady Gaga from what I heard. Tried to sue her for copyright but lost and ended up getting thrown out from her concert after storming the stage and trying to chew her face off. Anyway, can I have a snack?

Me: Only if you stop talking.

Crumb: Can I have a high in protein snack that's low in saturated fats?

Me: Yep.

Crumb: So a small high in protein, low in fat, squeaky snack?

Me: You're not eating any mice.

Crumb: I'll order a take-out then.

Me: You can't get a mouse take-out. Soup and a gravy one. Final offer.

Crumb: But I need to build my strength up!

Me: Then I'll make you some hearty soup.

Crumb: You can shove the hearty soup up your arse. We both know there's enough room there for a soup kitchen.

Me: *Takes out a chocolate mouse from a drawer and slowly licks it*

This is so sodding delicious. It's like they discovered what heaven tastes like and put it in a tasty treat!

Crumb: This ain't over.

Crumb flounces out, she's good at flouncing I'll give her that and I hear nothing else for half an hour. I'm starting to get worried. This is the correct response. I hear a knock on the door and I open it to find Crumb standing there wearing a trench coat, monocle and a stick-on moustache.

Crumb: Ah good morning. I believe you have pet mice, yes?

Me: Why yes, I do!

Crumb: Then it is your lucky day, for I am a world-famous mouse doctor and would like to offer your meeces a free health check.

Me: Well lucky, lucky me!

Crumb: Indeed. Can you kindly direct me to the mice?

Me: Of course, Doctor ... sorry I didn't catch your name.

Crumb: That's 'cus I didn't throw it at you, Chimpster.

Me: Did you just call me Chimpster?

Crumb: No, I was just clearing my throat. Cough Chimpster cough. See?

Me: Hmmmm ... So then, what is your name?

Crumb: My name? Erm it's …

I see her eyes darting from me to the hallway

Me: Take your time.

Crumb: It's …

Eyes once again go from me to the hallway

It's er ... fat bannister, yes that's it. Dr Fatbannister.

Me: *In my head I've just launched the little shit into space*

Well then come in esteemed Doctor.

Crumb: *Giggles quietly and mutters 'What An Idiot!'*

Me: Before you see the mice, may I ask about your credentials? Where did you study?

Crumb: College.

Me: Which one?

Crumb: Erm ...

Me: Can you not remember?

Crumb: Of course, I can. It's just that my brain is so massive and full of information that it takes a moment to locate certain things but I remember now. I studied at The College For Mice Doctors To Study At. It's a well-known and respected hall of learning.

Me: Never heard of it.

Crumb: Are you a mouse doctor?

Me: No.

Crumb: Exactly.

Me: Fair enough. Just one moment please.

I go into the kitchen, get the box of gravy bones and shake it loudly.

Me: Crumb, do you want a gravy bone?

Crumb: *Runs into the kitchen that fast I think she broke at least one world record*

Best give me just a small one 'cus I plan on filling up on mice ... Oh shit

Looks around wildly

Where am I?

Me: Shit Street, whippet.

Crumb: I have no idea what you're on about, I must have had a blackout due to my illness. I hope I didn't do anything out of character.

Me: Nope, everything was pure Crumb.

Crumb: Hmm. Anyhoo, I feel all weak ... think I need to have something to eat.

Me: Like a mouse?

Crumb: Now that you mention it, I could eat a mouse or two.

Me: Not happening Dr Fatbannister.

Crumb runs out the room and comes back in a poncho, sombrero and, hurrah, the stick-on moustache.

Me: *Puts head in my hands and asks God why, just why?*

Crumb: Hello, my name is ... Dr Chimptable and I am a famous Mexican psychiatrist.

Me: Do you speak Mexican, famous doctor?

Crumb: Arriba Arriba. That's Mexican.

Me: What does it mean?

Crumb: It means something in Mexican is what it means.

Me: Piss off Crumb.

Crumb: This is animal abuse. I'm setting my team of highly skilled and vicious lawyers on you.

Me: You don't have money for ONE lawyer, never mind a team of them.

Crumb: Can I borrow £5,000 for lawyers so I can sue your fat arse?

Me: You cannot.

Crumb: Testicles.

Whippet nap

Me: Hello Crumb.

Crumb: *Looking guilty*

Hello, you're back early.

Me: Yes, I see. What have you been up to?

Crumb: Nothing much, just having a read and a wap. Bit of yoga, despite the fact that I have no yoga pants and so had to do the Lotus position with my lady garden out.

Me: God help me and what's a wap?

Crumb: A whippet nap.

Me: Of course it is. So, have you been up to anything else? Maybe something that you wouldn't do had I been in the house?

Crumb: Nope, nothing I can think of, but can I say that you are looking very pretty today.

Me: Thank you. Are you trying to distract…

Crumb cuts me off again, she keeps doing this dammit!! She's so bloody hignorant.

Crumb: You truly are looking lovely on this bright sunny morn. You could be a model you really could.

Me: You aren't changing the subject?

Crumb: In fact, when you came in, I was like 'OMG it's Kate Moss!' You're practically glowing with beauty, like you have swallowed a small sun!

Me: Thank you very much, but what have …

Crumb cuts me off AGAIN, aaaarrrggghhh

Crumb: Radiant

Me: Radiant?

Crumb: Yes. If I had to choose one word to describe you, Radiant would be my first choice.

Me: You've been on the kitchen counter, haven't you?

Crumb: But I could have gone with so many others, for example, words I could have chosen include, but are not limited to, Stunning, Enchanting, Forgiving, Delightful, Alluring, Forgiving, Beauteous, Devine, Forgiving and so many more.

Me: I can see what you …

Crumb cuts in

Crumb: But I think I'm sticking with Radiant because that's what you are to me ... a ray of sunshine. Thank you, thank you for lighting up my life.

Me: Crumb, I know what …

Crumb: Radiant.

Me: Thank you, but …

Crumb: Like a fat Virgin Mary.

Me: Hmmmm ... Crumb, why have you got the mashed potato in front of you?

Crumb: OMG! How did that get here?

Me: I'm going to say that you jumped up on the counter, picked it up in your thieving mouth and then ate some and hoped you would have time to eat it and hide the evidence before I got home.? Any of that ringing a bell?

Crumb: No! You told me not to jump on the counter and I haven't. I am a truthful whippet; an honourable whippet and your accusations are besmirching my good name.

Me: Good name?

Crumb: I have a lot of ancestors and I imagine they are up in heaven listening to you as you sully our name. I bet they are talking about you now. Bet they are calling you unpleasant names. Names include, but are not limited to Cheapo von Chimpface, Chunky Monkey and Missy McTescovalueelectricblanketbuyer, that's because …

Me: Yes, yes, I got the hidden message in that one. So, if you didn't jump up, how did the mash get in between your paws?

Crumb: Well this is what I think happened, I was in the kitchen and the song Wind Beneath My Wings came on the radio and I started thinking how YOU were the wind beneath MY wings, and I'm not gonna lie, I got emotional because I care for you deeply. What must have happened is that my love for you, my wind, enabled me to grow actual wings and they must have picked me up and landed me on the bread bin.

Me: You flew?

Crumb: Only thing I can think of.

Me: And the mash?

Crumb: Must have taken it as proof that I flew. How else could I get it?

Me: You could have jumped up and stole it.

Crumb: Proof that my love for you can give this whippet wings and even move mountains …

*Clears throat and sings very, very loudly. *

Ohowowo la la la,

Did I ever tell you you're my hero?

Me: Oh sweet Jesus and his adoptive father please stop.

Crumb: *Again, singing**

You're everything I wish I could be,

Don't know the words so I'm improvising,

And somehow your bag is full of weeeee!

Me: *Gets up and heads towards the kitchen*

Crumb: Where you going?

Me: Probably prison.

Crumb: Does that mean you won't be needing those minty peas? Because they would go down smoother than a greasy hooker with this here mashed potato.

Me: *Bangs head on floor until death or unconsciousness turn up. Am happy to see either.*

Dial-a-Maul

I've woken up on Saturday to hear Crumb arguing with someone and I look out the window to find Crumb trying to grab a letter from the postman.

Crumb: Just give it me and I'll give it to her!

Postman: It has to be signed for; I've explained this!

He goes to knock on the door and Crumb jumps up and makes another attempt at getting the letter

Crumb: And I've explained that she's on holiday so can't sign for it, so pass it here and I'll make sure she gets it!

I decide to intervene. I go downstairs and open the door to find the postman holding off Crumb by holding her head while her front paws are windmilling around ineffectively.

Me: *I cough to get their attention. The postman looks relieved, Crumb not so much ... *

Crumb: You're back early, safe flight?

Postman: *Holds a letter out and a pen*

Letter for you, sign here and get your dog checked for rabies.

Me: *I sign the form and see Crumb legging it and think she is getting out the way because I've caught her lying about my whereabouts. I realise I am wrong when I hear what I can only describe as a War Cry and it's increasing in volume. I grab the postman and we both hit the floor as Crumb comes around the corner waving a samurai sword in each paw*

Crumb: AAARRRRGGGGGGHHHHHHHHHHHI'LLLLLLGIVE YOURABIESYOUMONUMENTALPRICK!!

Sees we aren't where she expected and tries to slow down but she's going too fast and so slams into the door

OWCHY! Oh, the pain!

Me: Oh shit, are you OK darling?

I pick her up and am amazed she is in one piece. I give her a hug.

Crumb: No, I'm not OK, I need medical attention. Please go and phone the vet!

Me: It will be quicker if I take you.

I run my hands over her and see no blood and make a note to thank God later

I start walking towards the car and feel her tense up. Are you alright? Where does it hurt?

Crumb: Please phone the vet, darling Fruitcake, just leave me here while you phone. I think I've broke my legs!

Me: OK Sweetie, back in a sec

I take my cardigan off and wrap her in it, kiss her and run to the phone but when I get to the door I realise my keys are in my cardi pocket and so I go to grab them and see that Crumb not wrapped up in my top, but is slowly walking towards the postman while balancing one of the swords on her paw

Crumb: I really fancy some fava beans ...

Me: CRUMB!

The postman sees his chance, chucks me the letter and bolts to his van.

Crumb: This ain't over, Pat! I'm getting you AND your little pussy!

Me: His name's Pedro, how do you know he's got a cat?

Crumb: *Sighs and runs her eyes with her paws in the manner of someone who is very weary*

Postman Pat, black and white cat? Shall I explain it again? Everyone knows the more you describe a joke the funnier it gets.

Me: Hmmmm

Opens the letter and sees it's a bill from Vistaprint. It has the word OVERDUE on it

Crumb!

Crumb: Yes, oh lovely, non-judgemental Fruitcake?

Me: Why have I got a bill from Vistaprint?

Crumb: Well I had an idea for a job and remember when I worked as a fortune teller?

Me: Yes, I do remember, I only finished paying the court fine last week.

Crumb: You don't like to let things go do you?

Me: I got a criminal record because of you, you felonious bell-end!

Crumb: If you're going to be living in the past can you at least do something useful and kill Hitler?

Sees my face and recognises the last few grains of sand are falling from her life's egg timer and decides to shut up

Me: So then, why have I got a massive bill?

Crumb: Are you a pelican? No? I feel I'm giving you some quality material here ...

Me: Why. Do. You. Owe. Vistaprint

Looks at the bill

£241?

Crumb: Technically, it's your name, so you do.

Me: CRUMB!

Crumb: Well I had a great idea for a business and they did some cracking work before so it made sense to go with them.

Me: What business?

Crumb: It's in the service industry and I would be offering a service that the average person couldn't afford until now.

Me: What service?

Crumb: Well it's for something you may want to buy for yourself or give as a gift to someone who is experiencing a problem.

Me: OK, this sounds like you've put thought into this. What service?

Crumb: Well you see, people sometimes come up against obstacles that they need help dealing with and that's where I come. Say, for example, that your neighbour keeps playing music late and it's keeping you up, yes?

Me: Go on.

Crumb: Well, he has asked politely but he laughs at you and the music gets louder, so he calls my Crumb Hotline and within 24 working hours the problem is solved.

Me: So you offer a mediation? Because that's already an established thing, it's not new, sorry darling.

Crumb: It's not what you would be able to put under traditional mediation, Fruitcake.

Me: OK tell me more.

Crumb: Well I could give you charts and projections, OR I could tell you the name and let it speak for itself. 3 words. Short. Sweet. To the point. I'll get you a poster later so you can see my vision but let me tell you the name of my company and let the name paint you a picture.

Me: OK, what's the name?

Crumb: Dial-A-Maul PLC.

Me: I'm going back to court, aren't I?

Crumb: More than likely.

Me: Fantastic.

Dial-a-Maul – the game plan

So, me and Crumb are in Starbucks and I'm having a hot chocolate and she's having a puppuccino, which is basically whipped cream in a pup-sized cup that she is really fond off. I promised her I would take her if she would help with the new pup and make her feel at home. When I found the pup logging on Amazon with my chewed up credit card in her paw, I realised that Crumb had indeed spent time with the pup and that I should know by now to attach a caveat to everything I ask her to do and no-one is to blame but me.

So we are having a chat about Dial-A-Maul ...

Crumb: So then, I'm thinking I need to start small …

Me: Good thinking.

Crumb: It's what I'm known for.

Me: *Mutters under my breath*

Not quite.

Crumb: See these?

Points to her ears

These can hear a crisp packet open in the bathroom while I'm downstairs watching the highly delectable

Judge Rinder and you're running the bath taps, so you don't have to share. I can, can't I?

Me: Yes. Yes, they can. I don't mind sharing but that's not enough for you ...

I stop as I can hear someone shouting in a horsey voice and wonder what the problem is. Then I hear what the problem is ...

Horsey woman: This is a Starbucks not Pets at Home, get that dog out of here!

I stand up and clear my throat

What's the problem?

Horsey woman: There's a dog in here.

Me: I'm aware of this. She's with me.

Horsey woman: I want it out!

Me: But even if we leave there will still be a bitch in here.

Horsey woman: *Narrows eyes*

This isn't a place for animals!

Me: But they serve a drink called a puppuccino. Puppuccino, so that means they allow pups in here. Just let me check something.

Looks at drinks menu

Hot chocolate, flat white, oh there it is, a twatty latte so that means that you must be welcome here too.

I feel a paw in my hand

Crumb: It's OK Fruitcake, I'll go. I know when I'm not wanted ...

At this point I would have slapped the miserable dickhead because Crumb looked so sad, but then I remembered this happened before in a cafe and while she did walk out it was only so she had a good run up to do a decent flying kick and so I decide she's up to something and we should probably leave. We get out and her dejected walk turns into a brisk one.

Me: What have you done?

Crumb: Let's go for an Indian head massage, my treat.

Me: But you have no money... you robbed her, didn't you?

Crumb: Shocked the thought entered your head, shocked!

Fans herself with a wad of £5 and £10 notes

May want to pick up the pace Fruitcake.

Me: She's going to notice that you nicked her money.

Crumb: I think when she opens her bag her mind will be on other things.

Grins

I hear a loud, very loud 'OH MY GOD!'

Crumb: Come on woman, shift it!

Breaks into a light trot

Me: Shat in her bag, didn't you?

Crumb: Maybe, it's a blur so I can't say for sure.

We get to my car and drive off. I was going to tell her off but what I did was to give her a high-five. We are both in a good mood when we stop at traffic lights. The light turns green and half a second later I hear a pip from behind me. I sigh and pull forward when the impatient sod pips again. I mutter 'Prick' and try to pull forward but we don't move. Crumb has put the handbrake on.

Me: Crumb what...

Crumb: *Holds up paw*

Shhh!

I see the bloke in the car has realised pipping isn't helping and is walking towards us.

Me: Crumb!

Crumb: Shhh!

The bloke bends down so that he is at my height. My current height, not the height I'll be when he kills me.

Man: What's your problem?

Crumb: Well when we were moving you pipped and when we stopped you pipped so I thought to myself: Let's stay put and when he comes over we can have a pow-wow, a little get together and see what the next move should be. Did I mention that I'm a judo black belt? If I didn't then I'm remiss because I should have mentioned it because that's what I am. A black belt.

He looks less angry and a tad more worried and Crumb picks up on this.

Crumb: *Lifts and kisses each front paw*

By law I should have a permit for these what with them being deadly weapons an all.

Now he is looking really worried.

Crumb: Heard of Osama Bin Laden?

Me: *Buries head in hands*

Crumb: Official story the army killed him. Unofficial story: Had a set of toothmarks to say he was shot. What's your name?

Man: *Looking very worried*

Er ... John.

Crumb: Nah, you look like a Kelvin.

Me: I know a couple of nice Kelvins.

Crumb: Kelvin …

Looks thoughtful

Kevin ... Swanfondler.

Kelvin Swanfondler: That's not my na …

Crumb: Did you say something, Swanfondler?

Kevin Swanfondler: No ... I'm going to go now, sorry for the misunderstanding

Starts to walk off

Crumb: Word of warning, Swanfondler. If I hear another pip, I'm coming for you. Even if it's not you pipping, you will be paying, you got that?

Waves her paw dismissively

Now bugger off.

After another high-five I put the car in gear but before I can move forward, I hear a pip from a car that's pulled up few cars behind us.

Crumb: *Unfastens her safety belt and leans out the window*

YOU DONE MESSED UP, SWANFONDLER!

Me: That wasn't his car.

Crumb: Doesn't matter. Gave my word. Going to chew his face

Gives me a quick lick and jumps out the car. I look behind me and see Swanfondler reversing VERY fast and screaming like he has caught his penis in a blender but Crumb's tail is wagging so she's having fun and that's the main thing xx

Furtato, and Crumb

Anyhoo, before the Furtato joined our family we only had one worry: Crumb.

She has her fair share of the 'Let's go kill and eat it!' gene in her so we were seriously concerned that she may treat her new sister like a light snack.

We were wrong.

On her second day with us, Lillie was crying as she was stuck upstairs. Crumb rushed up to find her and then she gently nudged her to get down.

Later, Lillie managed to knock the water bowl all over herself and cried, so Crumb licked her clean. She's even learned to play the whippet bitey face game with her new family!

(Unfamiliar with the bitey face game? Our pointy-nosed furries do this when playing. It can look fearsome and as though they're trying to bite the face off their furry friends and there's lots of snorting and rolling around, but it's a game, so all's well.)

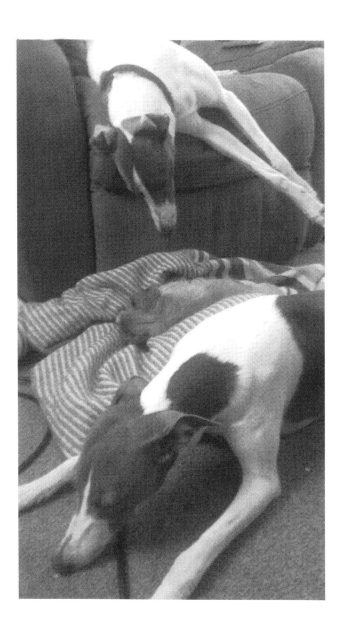

I watched with unaccustomed maternal pride when Furtato fell asleep. Titch moved on one side while Crumb lay with her head hanging over the chair and if Lillie made a sound, any sound, Crumb's eyes opened instantly.

I simply adore the whole lot of them.

Lillie was play fighting, she even climbed up on me and used me as a diving board.

It was sodding magnificent!

The ice-cream incident

Me: Crumb, have you stolen my dear nephew's ice-cream?

Crumb: Have you questioned the other whippets or just me?

Me: Not gonna lie, just you.

Crumb: This is discrimination! I share this substandard dwelling with three, count them, three other whippets and yet you always assume I'm the wrongdoer.

Me: Well to be fair, Crumbawumba, I asked you bec… hang on, substandard dwelling?

Crumb: Yes. Substandard. Hardwood floors and no hot tub, I may as well go live in the jungle or in the refugee camp in Calais.

Me: That can be arranged you sodding ingrate.

Crumb: We Whippets are not accustomed to slumming it. We are above the common groin sniffers that we are forced to mingle with at the park. We are strong yet delicate like a desert rose and should be treated thusly. I didn't want to bring up the lack of spa days, but you have forced my paw. I. Have. Never. Had. A. Spa. Day. I'm neglected.

Me: We bought you an electric blanket!

Crumb: It smells of piss.

Me: Because you pissed on it!

Crumb: Hello everyone and welcome to The Blame Game! Today's subject: Who can we blame for peeing on the Tesco value electric blanket, don't think I didn't notice that, you cheap prick.

Me: I saw you do it, you furry arsehole!

Crumb: Stop living in the past!

Me: It was last week.

Crumb: Still the past!

Me: Know what else is in the past?

Crumb: No but I bet you're still going to tell ...

Me: Going for a walk without having to apologise for a certain barky whippet who is all "BITCH I KEEEEL YOU!" while on the lead, but who hides behind me when there is nothing stopping you from going all Whippass on the other well behaved dogs.

Crumb: Was that really necessary?

Me: Was pissing on the blanket necessary?

Crumb: Touché.

Me: Now I'm going to ask this once more. Did you steal his ice-cream?

Crumb: I swear to God that I did not steal the ice-cream and ...

Me: Crumb …

Crumb: No please, let me finish. I admit to stealing in the past, but I have learnt from my mistakes and moved on and like to believe that my past has made me a better whippet. That's what life is about, learning and growing. So, I'm not perfect but I can say, paw on heart, that I didn't steal the ice-cream.

Me: It's still in your mouth.

Crumb: Well shit.

Sparkly Poo

Remember I said that this book is not for those fragile little fuckers who are easily upset or of a delicate nature. This and the next couple of chapters is why ...

To fill you in, yesterday a neighbour, who has access to the garden for bins, came to complain about dog poo on the garden. I pick the poo up every day but with four dogs there's going to be poo. They came around with an attitude, said they had photographed the poo and will return "To take more photos and escalate things on Wednesday". After a chat with SAS Commander Crumb, we decided (she decided and I agreed because she made several valid points. She had a pie chart. A pie chart!) … that if they were going to take pictures, then I was going to write 'Fuck Off' in poo. I wanted to write 'Go Fuck Yourselves' but I couldn't afford the KFC boneless bucket I would have needed for the extra letters.

Anyhoo, this morning Crumb woke me up. She had a paint splattered smock on and a French beret and was holding a palette knife.

Me: Dear, dear sweet Jesus what are you wearing?

Crumb: *Spins around*

You like? I'm an artist so I wanted to look suitably artistry.

Me: *It takes me a while for my brain to kick in*

Why are you an artist?

Crumb: We have an art project, remember? We are sculpting swear words in poo.

Me: Ah yes, still want to do that?

Crumb: Yes. I'm a Faecal Artist.

Me: I like it!

Crumb: Thank you. Come on then, let's have an Art Attack!

Me: Right then, I'll go collect the poo.

Crumb: What's that behind your ear?

Does a Derren Brown and produces a massive bag of poo from behind my ear

Ta-dah!

Me: You are a very special dog. Take that any way you want.

Crumb: Right then, first things first: We need to get an alibi. I have a friend who will swear it couldn't have been us that did it.

Me: An alibi?

Crumb: Yep. She will say that we nipped over for a coffee and then spent the morning working at a charity. She will swear on a stack of bibles that we were knitting beak cosies for elderly ducks.

Me: Beak cosies?

Crumb: Yes. I've made up some business cards with her phone number on it. I've gone on Wikipedia and made up a duck illness, Beak Frost: It's deadly, and a charity that makes beak cosies …

Hands over a small card

Me: *Reads card*

The charity is called Don't Kill Bill?

Crumb: Yes.

Me: How did you come up with that name?

Crumb: It came to me in a dream.

Me: I know I'm going to regret it but how did that happen? Explain the dream.

Crumb: Well I was dreaming about a duck warrior who's only weakness was a …

Me: A chilly beak …

Crumb: Holy shit! You had the same dream?

Me: Yes. It's spooky. Anyway, it's not illegal to swear poo, I don't need an alibi, I can't get arrested.

Crumb: It's not the police I'm worried about, it's your doctor.

Me: My doctor?

Crumb: Be honest, Fruitcake, you're one strike away from being able to head-bang the wall and not get a bruise.

Me: I'm ... well you see ... beak cosies you say?

Crumb: *Punches the air*

Let's go sculpt some shit!

Half an hour later we have managed to write Fuck Off in poo. If you think that's a long time, then YOU try it. I have no gloves so am using carrier bags and wondering what happened to my life.

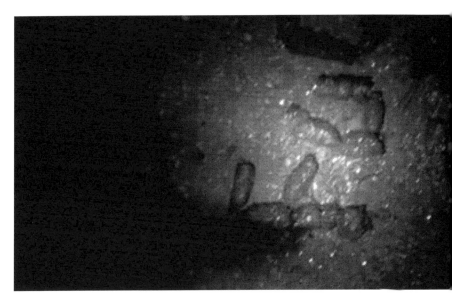

Crumb: *Looks critically at it*

I think it would look better in cursive script.

Me: Beg your pardon?

Crumb: Cursive. You know, joined up writing. You have lovely handwriting.

Me: When working in Ink, Whippet, in INK!

Crumb: I just think it could look more elegant that's all.

Me: We've written Fuck Off in whippet shit. We could dress it in Dior and it still wouldn't look classy.

Crumb: *Turn around to see she has magically changed from Artist into the camouflage outfit she wore yesterday in the War Room - aka the kitchen*

That sounds like a defeatist attitude soldier! Get down and give me fifty!

Me: I can give you half. Of a half. I mean I can lie down ...

Crumb: Where you from, Private Fruitcake?

Me: Ilkeston *aka* Beirut of the East Midlands.

Crumb: Only 2 things come from Ilkeston, Fruitcake, steers and queers and I can't see no horns!

Me: We can now add An Officer and A Gentleman to the Netflix blacklist.

Crumb: *Turns around and buggers off*

Me: Where you going?

Crumb: Remember when I said the thing about Fruitcake and steers?

Me: Yes. Do you feel bad? Are you going to hide your pointy face in shame?

Crumb: I am not.

Me: Where you going then?

Crumb: Kitchen.

Me: Why?

Crumb: 'Cus I now fancy a burger and some fruitcake.

Me: Silly me.

Poo aftermath

I just thought I'd share my memories as I took a short break from writing this book. I'd ask you not to tell Crumb that you're considering reporting her to the council over just one measly poo. I have too much time on my hands, she has too much time on her paws and has had a large McDonalds.

Tell me, what did you expect?

This is the letter I sent after they sent me a letter saying that they had seen a poo on the garden and would return in two days and take a pic of any poo. They also sent a shedload of papers about the dangers of dog poo.

Dear neighbours,

First of all, I need to apologise on behalf of my dog because it was her who wrote the sweary poo message. When I saw what she had done I was going to ground her but

A: She is a silent and cunning whippet who is adept at picking locks and so if she's got plans then there's sod all I can do apart from yelling CRUMB! CRUMB! like a fat female Marlon Brando in a Streetcar Named Desire while she legs it to the skatepark to meet the other canine delinquents.

But the main reason she wasn't grounded was B: I was impressed.

You may look at the photo you took of it and see a naughty word but I see something that took patience, skill and dexterity. My first thought was to add 'And The Horse You Rode On!' in my own waste but I couldn't do it, I just couldn't do it.

I got so far as an exclamation mark without a dot before realising that I simply didn't have the poise, balance or the poo to do it, basically I did a line and it wasn't even straight. Gutted doesn't begin to cover it.

Thank you for the pages and pages of information on the dangers of dog poo that you kindly, and with no thought to the environment, printed out. Nothing says I Am A Success In Life more than having access to a printer!

But here's the thing: I know dog poo is messy and not good for children which is why none of my nieces and nephews have ever received a box of it from me on their birthdays. When out with the dogs I clean up after them and even pick up other dogs' poo if I see it. I pick up the poo off the garden everyday but there's four dogs and even though I take them out several times a day sometimes they like to poo at home, I'm the same. I didn't have a bowel movement at work for 4 years. Sometimes they poo at night when I let them out before bed and if you think I'm going out there with a torch and a carrier

*bag at 10pm on a winter's night then welcome to the
town of Disappointmentville, population: You.*

*You will notice that I have printed out information for
you on the dangers of cat crap and this is because one of
your tenants had a cat which shat all over OUR garden
and yet I never saw them with a carrier bag on their
hand and a look on their face that told passers-by that it
was a dirty job but someone has to do it!*

*But maybe their hands were busy unwrapping fag
packets and leaving them in the alleyway which we
cleared up.*

*When taking the photos (the glitter was my idea. You're
welcome) you will have noticed that we had a
combination lock on the gate; HAD a combination lock
because late one night, one of your tenants kicked the
gate in and smashed the lock, but we understand, four
digits is so hard to remember.*

*I'm going to sign off in a moment because Crumb has an
audition for Britain's Got Talent tomorrow and she
wants to rehearse. She's going to, and without the use of
mirrors, attempt to write Ant & Dec on stage, so I need
to go get a KFC bargain bucket to provide her with the
raw materials. I'm so proud of her!*

*Basically, we want you to know that we spoke to the
council who said that as long as we weren't leaving the
poo for ages, they wouldn't take any action against us,*

and that unless it's bin day, you have no reason to be on our garden and that if we see you loitering there with a camera then we will call the police.

Toodles!

After a period of sober reflection, or perhaps not entirely sober, they DID return, they did take a picture and the council did a random spot check and they found no poo. Inexplicably, the pic of Sparkle Shit™ was sent around the various council departments where it gave many a stressed, overworked and underpaid worker a well-deserved laugh.

shit
glitter

Shit glitter. It's a little gold pill that will, yes, literally, make you shit glitter. This little pill is dipped in gold and filled with 24-karat-gold leaves and will make your poo all glittery and sparkling, at a price of US$425. If, you know, you are into that.

Tsunami of whippet shit

So then, I found that I had but £20 to last me all week. I thought, I know, I'll go buy the whippets a few treats. So, I left Poundland Plus with £3.95 after seeing a quilt and bed-in-a-bag on offer I thought they would love to snuggle in, plus some Jumbones. I spent £1 on myself, buying a cheap box of chocolates with a strawberry centre. £1. A whole frigging pound. Today I gave Crumb some extra ham as she had a tummy ache and needed to go outside a lot.

Crumb: Of woe is me!

Me: Are you OK darling?

Crumb: Yes, I'm fine. Woe is me is Latin for everything's tickety-boo.

Me: Is there any way that I can help, you sarcastic cretin?

Crumb: Ham?

Me: OK, but just a bit.

Crumb: Just a bit? Just a sodding bit? I could be dying and ham could be the cure that you're depriving me!

Me: Crumb, if you have runny poos then you need to just eat lightly and you will feel better sooner than if you're chowing down on a pound of ham.

Crumb: I don't have runny poos!

Me: Crumb, you've been outside every half hour since early this morning.

Crumb: That's because it's such a lovely day.

Me: It's pissing sleet, Crumb. Just admit you've got the runs, it's not a big deal.

Crumb: How dare you? My stools are firmer than my thighs!

Attempts to do a star jump but stops halfway and a pained expression comes over her pointy face.

Me: Are you OK? Do you need to go outside?

Crumb: Nope!

Me: Crumb, why are you denying it? Have you eaten something you shouldn't have …?

Crumb: Slander!

Me: Oh God what have you eaten?

Crumb: All you do is ask questions! Let's change places, shall we? When did YOU last have a poo, and how was its consistency?

Me: This morning, and I was shocked it wasn't like water considering that you hid in the bathroom dressed like a vampire and then jumped from behind the shower curtain when I was just getting nice and relaxed. Having a bowel movement in peace and solitude is on my bucket list. Crumb, you really look like you need to go outside …

Realises that I have one thing in the house that's mine

Where are my strawberry chocolates?

Crumb: You always assume the worst don't you, Missy Von Assumer?

Me: Crumb, I had one bloody treat! Can I not have one treat?

Crumb: Chocolatey ones? No. But if you want a REAL treat then I will perform an interpretive dance where, through graceful movement and facial expressions, I will explain the story of the English Civil War. Sit back while I, Crumb, the Darcey Bussell of whippets takes you on a rollercoaster ride through our country's dark and bloody past! Now, this takes place over several years, but I've got it down to an 8-hour performance. Get some popcorn and chocol… OK get some popcorn and experience the mammoth opus that is Crumb's Civil War.

Me: I'll give you all the ham to stop this.

Crumb: Too late, I'm feeling all educational. Now before I start you need to know a few little-known facts about the Civil War. First, that Oliver Cromwell was skilled at the high kicking routine familiar to Vegas show girls.

Me: Oh God ...

Crumb: And secondly, Charles The First was a black belt in Judo who has mastered the art of levitation. Ready?

Me: Oh Sweet Jesus and all his angels, No.

Crumb: I'm taking that as an Alternate Yes

She starts off with her head bowed like she is praying and then launches into the Can-can. Unfortunately this movement is more than her stomach can take, and in protest, it releases its contents and Crumb manages to defecate in a 5 foot arc that passes over the table and telly before smashing into the Welsh dresser with such force that it shatters a tea set that stood unblemished through two world wars but was unable to defend itself against a tsunami of liquid whippet shit.

FINE! I admit It! I ate your chocolates. You were right, OK, I ate them! Are you happy?

Flounces off like a turkey on a Segway

Me: *Looks around to see poo running down the walls, about 300 pieces and 5000 splinters of crap-drenched crockery and evil smelling smoke coming from the back of the T.V.*

Crumb: *Pokes her head around the door while holding a half empty box of Jaffa cakes*

Well are you!?

Me: Are you eating Jaffa cakes!?

Crumb: I'm feeling all weak because although it may have escaped your notice, I've very recently been ill. But on the bright side, you were right and so enjoy your victory. Happy?

Me: No.

Crumb: Then I don't feel bad about bringing you down if you're already there, but it appears someone has shit on your bed ...

The Microsoft man

So yesterday I came in as the phone was ringing. Crumb padded over and picked it up.

Crumb: *Listens for a few seconds then puts call on hold*

Fruitcake, an Indian man called Kevin says he's from Microsoft. Are we having problems with the internet?

Me: No hon, it's a scam.

Crumb: Really?

Me: Yep. They get you to follow their instructions on your computer and then charge you for work they haven't done. If you followed their instructions, they have access to your computer and can rob you again by nicking your details.

Crumb: You're shitting me?

Me: No hon, put the phone down.

Crumb: *Holds up a paw*

I could put the phone down …

Me: But you're not going to, are you?

Crumb: *Grins and shakes her head. She takes the call off mute and puts it on speakerphone. When she speaks her voice has changed and now she sounds like a Scottish octogenarian reminiscent of Robin Williams in Mrs Doubtfire*

Oh hello dearie! My great grandson says you want to speak to me about my computer. I hope there isn't a problem because I'm old and easily confused. Oh my poor back and isn't the youth of today lazy?

"Kevin": Yes, they are. Now the reason we are calling you …

Crumb: Make the bone-idle sods join the army!

"Kevin": Yes indeed. Now then ...

Crumb: I have a feeling we will need more troops too as I'm starting to get a bad feeling about this Hitler bloke. Don't like the cut of his jib.

Me: Cut of his jib? Jesus Christ ...

Crumb: *Turns around and whispers*

Piss off Fruitcake, I'm busy!

Goes back to talking to "Kevin"

I don't trust the man; he could get all invasive and where would I be then?

"Kevin": Oh, I understand. Now then, turn your computer on ...

Crumb: Up Shit Creek is where we will be Kevin! I don't know about you but I can't go to the shops without my mobility scooter and inhaler so if he wants me to goosestep everywhere, we are going to have a problem, aren't we?

"Kevin": No need to worry yourself madam.

Crumb: Easy to say when it's not your arse that's surplus to requirements. He could put me in pies!

Me: *Buries face in hands*

"Kevin": So then, just turn your computer on ...

Crumb: Oh, those words bring back the memories, my dear sweet dead husband could turn me on, light a lamp!

"Kevin": That's nice Madam. Is your computer on?

Crumb: It was better than nice Kevin, it was bleeding spectacular.

"Kevin": I'm pleased for you, now then …

Crumb: Not as pleased as me, that man could play me like a harmonica.

"Kevin": Get Google up ...

Crumb: We both had little signs that we would give each other when we were in the mood.

"Kevin": Is your computer on at all?

Crumb: All he had to do was to raise his eyebrows and I would slide off my chair.

Me: Dear sweet Jesus please stop.

Crumb: Right off my chair I tells you!

"Kevin": So, type the following into the search bar.

Crumb: Very spontaneous when it came to the arts of love, he really was.

"Kevin": Please listen and do what I tell you.

Crumb: But don't think it was all that way. We had a regular thing going on Sunday. When the credits to Songs of Praise came my heart started racing because I knew he was going to bend me over the hostess trolley and give me a pounding not dissimilar to what happened to the beaches of Normandy in '44.

"Kevin": Are you listening at all?

I can hear the first crack in his voice

Crumb: It's taking a minute to load. So then, a real good lover was my husband, built like a Grand National winner.

"Kevin": Please ...

Crumb: Monday morning I was always walking like I'd been fingered by the Hulk.

"Kevin": Please ...

Crumb: Not complaining mind you, and it wasn't really a problem. Looking back the only issue I would have had was if I needed to catch a pig in a passageway but that never occurred.

"Kevin": OK, I'm going to ask a colleague to call you back as we seem to be having difficulty.

Crumb: Oh, that's a shame, I was hoping we could sort it now. My wealthy grandson has given me his platinum credit card to use for emergencies. Would you say that this is an emergency?

"Kevin": *Sounding a lot more upbeat*

Platinum you say?

Crumb: Yes. It's the one with no limit because my wealthy son is wealthy.

"Kevin": I've just had a thought.

Crumb: Really? What was that thought?

"Kevin" That because you are vulnerable and elderly, I really should get this sorted today.

Crumb: You're so kind, young man.

"Kevin": I have a mother too.

Crumb: And I bet you are a wonderful son. Let me just put my specs on. Right then, what do I do?

"Kevin": Go to the search bar.

Crumb: I can't, my scooter's in the shop.

"Kevin": It's not a real place, it's on the top left-hand

screen.

Crumb: I found it! Call me Sherlock Holmes!

"Kevin" Well done. Now type in 'Micro 34885 AZ' and press send.

Crumb: Oh my God! Why Kevin, why?

"Kevin" What is the problem?

Crumb: Its porn Kevin! Oh, sweet Jesus, I never even saw this many ballsacks when I worked in a sport shop!

"Kevin": That should not happen. Try again.

Crumb: I don't know if I dare!

"Kevin": You must have pressed a wrong key. I shall repeat it so listen closely. Micro 34885 AZ.

Crumb: AHHH!

"Kevin": What now?

Crumb: There's a naked man on the screen and he's trying to insert his penis into his own bum, Oh the humanity!

"Kevin" It shouldn't do that. Try again.

Crumb: He's speaking! Shall I tell you what he is saying?

"Kevin": Yes. Something isn't right.

Crumb: He's saying 'I know you're not from Microsoft and that you are trying to scam me, so why not follow my lead and go fuck yourself'

*Puts down the phone *

I just high fived my whippet.

Fortune telling

Me: Crumb, do you know why I have a bill from the printers for £135?

Crumb: Oh that's for my printing. You said I could do it.

Me: No, I sodding didn't!

Crumb: You did, you told me, and I'm quoting here, "Crumb, I am not working as a prostitute in order to buy you a bespoke coat. You want one? Earn it!"

Me: Where in that sentence did I say you can run up a huge bill at the printers? Can you point it out as I'm unable to locate it?

Crumb: It was inferred.

Me: Please explain how.

Crumb: You said I needed to earn some money and I saw a programme on Psychics and thought, I can do that, and so I had the printers run up a 1000 of these.

Goes to her bed and brings over a crumpled poster

What do you think?

Me: You're not psychic!

Crumb: I KNEW you were going to say that! Spooky, eh?

Me: Are you shitting me, whippet?

Crumb: Nope. I have a rare and special gift.

Me: For the love of God, you're serious, aren't you?

Crumb: Yes. God blesses few with the gift of clairvoyance and I have been fortunate enough to be given such a gift. I hope I can guide people through the maze that is life's journey with my knowledge of the future. In return for money.

Me: Crumb, I hate to break it to you, but people aren't going to hand over their hard-earned money to a psychic dog.

Crumb: Well unless being wrong is your New Year's Resolution I have some bad news for you.

Goes back to her bed and returns with a small purse

Take a shufti at that.

Me: *Opens purse to see it stuffed with coins and several £10 notes*

How the bloody hell did you get this?

Crumb: I told you, I tell people their future and if they don't like what I am foretelling then I can help change the future. For money.

Me: OK, pretend I am your client and go through this step by step.

Crumb: I can, but using my power is draining mentally and physically. I will need something to give me the strength to push open the curtains that separate the now from the tomorrow. I seem to recall a sirloin steak poking out the shopping bag ...

Me: Not happening.

Crumb: *Puts one paw on her forehead while the other paw is flailing about*

I'm trying to do it ... but I'm too weak ... the future ... 'twill not reveal itself ... need ... more ... power!

Me: For fucks, fine!

Gets steak from fridge and reluctantly passes to the pointy-nosed Mystic Meg who seems to swallow it without chewing

Oh much better! Right then, I will go up to a person and hand them a poster and offer to tell their future.

Me: OK, then what?

Crumb: They usually tell me to piss off.

Me: Understandable.

Crumb: Shall I carry on? Or are you planning to let me speak, Missy McInterrupto?

Me: Sorry, please continue.

Crumb: So after they tell me to piss off, I offer them a glimpse into their future.

Me: What, exactly, do you say?

Crumb: I explain that unless they give me some money, in the very near future someone will break into their homes and poo in their fridge.

Me: *Buries head in hands*

That's blackmail, you stupid furball!

Crumb: I have heard that word before, but ungifted people often throw harsh words at those whom God has bestowed second sight.

The doorbell starts ringing frantically. I go to the door and find two policemen who ask if they can have a word

Me: Yes of course, come in. How can I help you?

Policeman 1: We have had several complaints from your neighbours who have informed us that someone here is running a fake psychic company and that they are being blackmailed into handing over money. Do you know anything about this?

Me: It's not me, it's my dog! She had been bugging me to buy her a bespoke coat and I've explained many times that I can't afford to but that she should earn her own money and she's come up with this idea to get money! I know nothing about it!

Policeman 2: Clearly you do or you wouldn't be able to explain it to us, no?

Me: Well yes, but she's literally just told me about it when I asked her to explain a bill from the printers.

Policeman 1: So you are saying that this whippet came up with this idea, got leaflets printed and then threatened people with shitting in their shoes if they didn't hand over cash?

Me: Yes! Crumb tell them what you told me!

Crumb: *Tilts head*

Me: Crumb, I'm serious! I can go to prison for this! Tell them it was your idea to blackmail our neighbours because you want a bespoke coat, tell them!

Crumb: Woof

Me: Oh, you Motherfucker.

Crumb's Cosplay

So, Crumb has been bugging me to lend her my credit card as she wants to buy a bespoke Princess Leia outfit. When I said I would only lend it her when Satan was figure skating in Hell, she decided to try another tack.

Crumb: Did you know it was me who found your unconscious and drugged-out self?

Me: I thought it was my sister.

Crumb: No. 'Twas me.

Me: Casey said when she found me you were snoring. She also told me that when the paramedics said that I was dying you asked them that if I DID die, could they kindly blow some air into me and then seal my airways shut so you could use my corpse as a Lilo at the seaside.

Crumb: LIES! I would NEVER say something so crass!

Me: Then you buggered off upstairs.

Crumb: I'm being slandered! I said no such thing. I held your hand and never left your side!

Me: Paramedics have bodycams. I can find out what happened easily enough.

Crumb: *Rubs her temples with her paws looking pained*

Hang on, to quote Celine Dion, it's all coming back to me.

Me: Thought it might.

Crumb: I was so devastated at the thought of losing you that ... erm, I ...

Me: Take your time.

Crumb: This is a very traumatic memory! So ... I was so upset at the thought of losing you, my little stoned simian, that I couldn't live without you ... yeah that might work ...

Me: I don't think you meant to say the last bit out loud.

Crumb: Shut your face, I'm in the middle of a flashback here! So, anyhoo, I was so bereft at the thought of you dying and that I couldn't live without you, this way I could still make memories with you. I thought I could take you someplace quiet, a lake, or someplace serene and beautiful where I could re-live the good times that I have had with you, and that I could grieve while holding your cold hand.

Me: That is indeed a very touching.

Crumb: Yes it is.

Me: I feel like shedding tears.

Crumb: Understandable. Tissues are in the kitchen and if I was you, I would be giving me the steak you have for Richard's dinner because he didn't find you and raise the alarm.

Me: Richard isn't really a doggie person. He likes whippets in general but it's you that he took the police on a forty-mile trip around Matlock Bath.

Crumb: It was very scenic.

Me: Well his car wasn't by the time he got it back.

Crumb: Not my problem if the sheep threw mud at the car!

Me: We're going to back to the alarm raising in a moment but I have another quick question for you.

Crumb: Is it "Do you want to be nominated for a Pride of Britain Award?" because the answer is yes, but you will need to give me your credit card because if I turn up in something cheap, then people will be disgusted that Chimp (whose life I saved) hasn't sprung for a decent dress and will probably throw large rocks at you. David Walliams looks like he has a good aim. That your question?

Me: Sadly, that's not what I was going to ask you, so let's shelve Pride of Britain for the time being and let's talk about something else.

Crumb: Is it "Why do you deserve such a loyal furry friend?" 'cus the answer is you don't if we're going on the heroic act v steak content of my food. Sorry but it needs saying, and talking of steak, why aren't I chewing one while you re-live my kindness?

Me: I wondered why you would run upstairs while I was in that state.

Crumb: I went upstairs to pray for you to be bought back to us and it's closer to heaven.

Me: So, you didn't use my computer?

Crumb: No. I was too busy beseeching God to save you.

Me: I looked at the computer history and found you logged in while I was out of it. What's this Crumb?

I hold out a piece of paper

Crumb: *Stares at the paper for a good solid minute and I can see the cogs in her head working rapidly*

I swear by any God you fancy that I've never seen it before.

Me: This was what was written on the computer at the time the ambulance was here. Shall we read it together?

Crumb: No.

Me: OK, I'll read it alone. It says, "Crumb Dog Millionaire presents! Come party on the floating Chimp! Join me, The Crumb, as we dance and smoke a lil' dope while taking this monkey down the rapids at The Heights of Abraham! £15 per head payable to Crumb. No refunds."

Crumb: I must have done that while in a mental fog caused by the stress. I'm just asking a question here, but have you heard of multiple personality syndrome?

Me: Yes, and you don't have it.

Crumb: Are you sure?

Me: Yes.

Crumb: Bugger.

Me: Can we go back to why you didn't call an ambulance when you saw that I was not only dancing with death but had gone to his house after, got drunk and let him finger me?

Crumb: I probably am going to need surgery to get that out my mind's eye so thanks for that. Going back to the question asked, I knew the kids (furries) were sleeping, so I telepathically told your sister you were in trouble.

Me: Why didn't you just quietly tell her, or, and I believe this is a very valid question, why didn't you get off your furry arse and call an ambulance yourself?

Crumb: *Looks at her watchless paw*

My God is that the time? I'm late for cosplay!

Me: You don't have an outfit.

Crumb: I'll just go as a whippet

Legs it out the door then about 10 seconds later she comes in, puts a paw on each shoulder and licks my nose ever so gently

I love you and I'm glad you're not dead.

Turns around and runs to the door

Sees you later alligator!

Me: *Sighs*

Hang on a sec

I run upstairs and come down with a Princess Leia outfit

Crumb: You're supposed to say 'In a while crocodile'

She sees the outfit and actually squeals

ILOVEYOUILOVEYOUILOVEYOU!

She puts it on and when she's dressed I give her a light sabre

I'm off to save the universe, wish me luck for the fate of Chimpdom rests on my furry shoulders!

She blows me a kiss then runs out the door

Reluctantly, I go to do some cleaning and I plan to watch Breaking Bad that I'd saved. When I turn the telly on I find Crumb has deleted it and all I can find is Judge

Rinder. She's such a dick. I wait up for her and about 1 a.m. I hear her come in. She usually sneaks in and swears blind she came in before dark but not this time.

Crumb: Yo Fruitcake! Wake up and get me that steak for I have saved us!

Me: Had a good time?

Crumb: Are you listening? I have saved you all! Chuck us that steak and I'll give you the story. I imagine the press will be banging on the door and offering me millions to exclusively tell them my tale of Derren Brown do!

Me: I think you mean Derring-do.

Crumb: No I don't.

Me: *Rubs my eyes and as always in these situations, I ask myself "Why didn't I just have kids instead*

OK, tell me what happened.

Crumb: Well, after a drink and much debate, it was decided that I fight Darth Vader. I knew if I failed that the universe would go to the dark side and so I took my light sabre and hit him, but it was faulty and didn't slice him like I expected ...

Me: *I start to feel worried. Surely she knows it's all play acting. Please God let her know this*

Crumb: And so, I was there with a faulty weapon and no way to fight him. What was I to do?

Me: Did you concede defeat? Yes? Please say yes.

Crumb: *Ignores me completely*

But then I channelled Bear Grylls and thought 'Improvise, Adapt and Overcome', so I picked up a bar stool and twatted him around the head with it!

Me: Oh dear sweet baby Jesus ...Is he alright?

Crumb: I fucking hope not!

Me: Do you know what cosplay means?

Crumb: I'm assuming it's Latin for Fight To The Death. Anyhoo, the victor is getting the steak then having a long shower. Need to be fresh for the parade they're going to throw for me. Night night, Fruitcake.

Me: Night night. Crumb.

I'm going to pack my toothbrush and just wait for the police to fetch me.

Britain's Got Talent

Crumb: Get dressed, I have an announcement to make.

Me: When you say you have an announcement; I always feel a tidal wave of dread wash over me.

Crumb: Dramatic little chimp, aren't you?

Me: I go by experience.

Crumb: Bit judgemental if you don't mind me saying so.

Me: I have something called a memory.

Crumb: You're such a wuss.

Me: But when you make your little announcements it never ends well for me, why is that Crumb?

We go into the front room and I see the other four dogs in Bohemian Rhapsody formation. Why does my dog do this? I've never seen a French Bulldog pull this kind of crap.

Crumb: Right then, I wish to make an announcement …

She points to the other whipplets who start no sing a very nice a cappella version of Rule Britannia

Me: I need to get a job so I'm out the house more 'cus this isn't normal.

Crumb: Shut your face. Right then, I have something to say and you are going to be awed so please prepare for that.

Me: I'll try my best, now kindly get on with it.

Crumb: I have decided that I am going to work at the airport as a search dog. I love this country.

Pulls a flag from God knows where and waves it

Britain is under attack and I, The Crumb, will use my nose, my forensic knowledge...

Me: Forensic knowledge? You mean you've watched the crime channel?

Crumb:
ANDEEEEEEEEEEEWILLALWAYSLOVEYOOOOO
OOOOOOOOOOOOOOOOOOOOOOO
HAVEYOUFINISHEDINTERRUPTING?LOVE
YOOOOOOOOOOOOOOOOOOOOOOTHISISTHEL
ONGPLAYVERSIONLOVE
YOOOOOOOOOOOOOOOOOOOOOOOOOOOOOO
OEYEEEEEEYYYYYYYYEEEEELOVEYOOOOOO
OOOOOOOOOOOOOOOOOOOOOOOOOOOOOOO
OOOOOOOOOOOO

ME: For the love of all that is holy please stop.

Crumb: Any more interruptions and I'm moving on to Saving All My Love For You. You've been warned. Anyhoo, I have decided that I will be the one thing that defends Britain from the evil doers. I shall sniff out explosives but will specialise in finding drugs.

Me: *Holds up hand*

I'm not interrupting but I have a question.

Crumb: You may ask it.

Me: You're so kind. You know that dogs at the airport don't get paid?

Crumb: For shame! Hang your head! I require no remuneration for this! The feeling that I will get from finding the bad guys will be my payment. While I cannot put it in the bank, it will make me rich in my heart! I'm shocked, yes shocked, that you could think I would ask for money!

Me: I'm so sorry. Please forgive me.

Crumb: I shall forgive you but we will need a steak to make it right.

Me: Not a problem.

Crumb: Then we shall move past the insult. Anyhoo, I shall use my nose in defence of the country that I love so much.

Me: That's wonderful and I am in awe of your passion.

Crumb: That's only to be expected.

Me: This is true. You do know that any drugs you sniff out are taken to a locked unit that's not accessible to the dogs AND the dogs are both searched before leaving and take a blood test to make sure you don't take drugs with you.

Crumb: What?

Me: You heard me.

Crumb: Are you shitting me, Chimp?

Me: Nope!

Crumb: *Throws flag at me and stalks off*

Me: *I'm laughing so hard it hurts*

But Britain! The fate of this great country!

Crumb: Oh bugger off!

Me: Such a patriot. God I love my dawg!

Photos for Judge Rinder

I got a surprise in the post today ...

Me: Crumb? Cruuumb? CRUMB!

Crumb: *Head pops from behind the sofa. She has a towel turbaned on her head and she has her body and face covered in what looks like pink goo*

How may I help you?

Me: I've got a letter from Nottingham County ... is that my face mask?

Crumb: No.

Me: OK, well I've got a letter and ... it looks like my face mask.

Crumb: It isn't.

Me: Alright, well when you borrowed my car apparently ... hang on a sec ...

Goes to bathroom and returns with an empty pot of face mask

That's my face mask! You nicked my face mask!

Crumb: I borrowed it, massive difference. I know you know the difference as you used to have a dictionary. I know this because I've got it.

Me: Borrowed means you will give it back.

Crumb: And I will, I'll scrape it off and put it back in the pot and happy Chimp! I said Happy Chimp.

Me: I heard.

Crumb: *Stage whispers*

Then you probably want to tell your face.

Me: You're not scraping it back in the pot.

Crumb: That's what I usually do.

Me: What?! Were those your hairs in it?

Crumb: Yes. Think of them as a natural exfoliant.

Me: You said they were Thai keratin worms! You're a liar.

Crumb: I'm going to be honest and say I think that says more about your intelligence than it does about me.

Me: You owe me a new face mask.

Crumb: Yeah, that's not gonna happen. Oh I have a great idea! Why not take me on Judge Rinder!

Me: Not taking you on Judge Rinder.

Crumb: Oh go on! Imagine this: He gives me a Bible to swear on and I bow my head all demurely but raise my eyes and smile swiftly before going back to demure.

Me: Demure? You?

Crumb: Yes, demure!

Me: I'll believe it when I see it.

Crumb: You will see it, Judge Rinder.

Me: Not going on Judge Rinder.

Crumb: Not listening. So we both swear on the Bible and then I state my case so cleverly while you stutter, so I basically thrash you and am awarded £5000.

Me: Imaginative dog aren't you.

Crumb: Shut up and picture this: As we leave the court, Judge Rinder brushes up against me and apologises, and yet I see something in his eyes.

Me: One of your dog hairs?

Crumb: Sod off! It's desire, pure nekked want. He gently pats my head and strokes my soft furry face. He tells me I feel like silk. I blush daintily. Had he stroked your hair he would dislodge flakes of pastry.

Me: I hate you with the fire of a thousand suns.

Crumb: Backatcha dipshit. He comments on my smooth silky fur and asks if he can take me to dinner. Shyly, I accept. We go to The Ivy where he tells me he has feelings for me as we down oysters. He takes my paw and asks if we can go to his place for coffee. I accept, but coffee is never drunk, because as soon as we are in the door, we are ripping each other's clothes off.

Me: Oh dear God.

Crumb: Oh the things we do! He really learnt some moves on Strictly and has me doing things that will shock a dock whore!

Me: I will give you a fiver to stop talking.

Crumb: I'll be lying there thinking, "Will this pleasure ever end!"

Me: I feel dirty, your words are sullying me.

Crumb: If I recall correctly, Benedict Cumberbatch is a close friend.

Me: *Holds up fiver*

Not sure where this is going but I'm starting to worry ...

Crumb: Do you reckon he would be up for one of those mengy twa things? Oh to be the meat in that sandwich!

Me: AH! AH! AH!

Puts fingers in ears

Lalalalalala! I can't hear you!

Crumb: I could do a kiss and tell with The Sun newspaper and earn some cash. Probably going to wear a black basque for my photo. The readers will then understand the pure naked arousal that I elicit in Rinder and Cumberbatch. Probably need to carry a warning as my photo will cause lesbians to slide off their chairs and males to cover unbridled erections.

Me: Can we please go back to what I was talking about?

Crumb: Was we talking about how, if you get any fatter, we are going to have to grease you up to get you through doorways?

Me: Frig off. I have a £60 fine for driving on a tram only road. I haven't driven on a tram road. Your dealer lives near a tram road.

Crumb: I don't have a dealer; I am merely high on life.

Me: I don't think high on life means you eat 3 pizzas, a pack of ginger biscuits and giggle at the telly for 5 hours when it's turned off. You owe me £60 and a face mask.

Crumb: Can you just...

Me: Not going on Judge Rinder.

Crumb: Bollox.

Oh McDonalds!

Crumb: Oh McDonalds!

Me: Yeah! It's not for you.

Crumb: But I'm hungry.

Me: Shame. But you're not having any.

Crumb: Alright.

Me: Really?

Crumb: No. Gimme a fry. One. Single. Fry.

Me: No.

Crumb: But I will leave you alone after that. You won't see me, I'll be like Keyser Söze in tonight's film: Silence Of The Crumb.

Me: I don't believe you .

Crumb: Oh that hurts!

Me: Oh I'm sorry. Would you say that hurts as much as standing up to find a waggy tailed cretin has hidden a piece of chewed up Lego in your shoe, or less? Because that really hurt. I thought I was having a heart attack in my fucking foot.

Crumb: I have no recollection of that.

Me: I have no recollection of the French Revolution, yet they still don't have kings.

Crumb: Ah yes, the French Revolution. Started over a small item of food, not dissimilar to a McDonalds' fry ...

Me: Fine! *Reluctantly hands over one fry*

Crumb: Lovely! There's someone at the door.

Me: OK, back in a second

Goes to door, sees no one and returns to Crumb head first in my nephew's happy meal. Something that is ironically making him very unhappy

CRUMB!

Crumb: You rang?

Me: Stop stealing his food!

Crumb: Not my fault because ...

Me: It's YOUR head in the box!

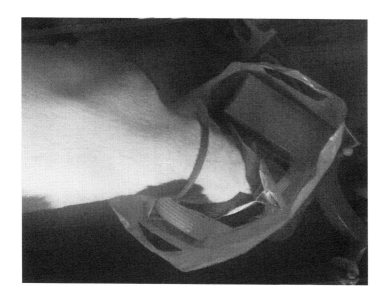

Crumb: As I was saying before I was rudely interrupted, I was watching the Crime Channel and did you know that not one of the criminals ever mentioned spa days!? A coincidence? Probably. But to be sure let's see if a hot stone massage will curb my thieving ways.

Me: I'm cancelling Sky.

Crumb: Can you wait 'til the morning. Since I've been denied a bespoke coat or a stylist, I'm looking at other options for my look. According to the T.V. guide there is a programme on canine fashion tonight.

Me: You're making that up.

Crumb: Cross my heart. It's called Doggy Style and it's on the Adult Channel.

Me: Oh God ...

Father Francis

When I go out with Crumb I've noticed that people are looking at us differently. Usually they look at us with confusion because their brain is telling them that if they added a moustache to the whippet, it would look just like the 'Bank employee' who came to their house, asked them to confirm their bank card details and who scarpered pretty fucking sharpish when asked for ID.

Luckily people tend to ignore their brain when it does this due to the fear that asking a whippet if they had dressed up in a suit and tried to scam them, is a small step on a long road, one that ends with them wearing knickers on their head and telling the world that they are the reincarnation of Abraham Lincoln and no one needs that.

[If these sentences are long, pity me, I'm out of breath.]

But recently, the looks have changed from recognition tinged with accusation to smiles and even a hat tip from elderly gentlemen.

Had I been new to Crumb I would have thought that she had had a change of heart and decided to be good and help those in the community but I'm not new to Crumb and so my 'Crumb Being A Dick To Somebody' sense is tingling. I've just nipped into a shop and as I came out I saw an old lady talking to Crumb. She didn't call her

Crumb; she called her Father Francis before wandering off.

Me: What's going on?

Crumb: I have absolutely no idea what you are on about.

Me: That lady seemed to think you were a priest.

Crumb: Oh that? No. She merely confused me with someone else, a simple misunderstanding.

I can believe that, the lady was in her 80's and had glasses on. We carry on shopping and no less than 4 people have referred to my whippet as Father Francis. They smiled at her and this is not only unusual it's worrying.

Me: What's going on?

Crumb: I think I must have a doppelganger. Only explanation I can think of.

Me: Hmmmm.

Crumb: Can you think of another reason?

Me: No, but that doesn't mean I'm buying your explanation.

Crumb: I am hurt. What have I ever done to deserve your lack of faith?

Me: Stole my bank card and bought 3 tonnes of high end dog treats. Told me someone was at the door then when I went to answer it you nicked my pizza. Flooded the house after watching The Titanic and then tried to drown your sister. Robbed our neighbour on many occasions ...

Crumb: It was a rhetorical question you arsehole!

We head home in silence and I'm beginning to think she was telling the truth. Not because I believe her but because I can't think of another reason.

Me: I'm sorry.

Crumb: Beg your pardon?

Me: I'm sorry.

Crumb: What exactly are you sorry for?

Me: You know for.

Crumb: Let's pretend I don't.

Me: I'm sorry that I thought you were up to mischief but I was wrong.

Crumb: Say that last bit again.

Me: *Breaths deeply*

I was wrong.

Crumb: One more time for those at the back.

Me: Don't push it, whippet. I'm sorry.

Crumb: And so you should be

Puts her paw on her forehead and sighs dramatically

Your harsh words have pierced my soul and left me wounded.

Me: *I see we are coming to the butchers*

If I gave you some money to buy a steak would that help with your recovery?

Crumb: Shall we try?

Me: *Hands over a £20 note*

I'll wait here.

Crumb darts off to the shop and returns with a steak the size of her head. She breathes it in and in less than as minute it's gone.

Me: Better?

Crumb: Much better!

Me: Do I get change?

Crumb: You do not.

We're halfway home when I see a middle-aged couple coming over. They look like they recognise Crumb and so I think that her doppelganger story must be true and resolve to buy her another steak for my not believing her. However, my money stays in my pocket ...

Man: Ah good morning Father!

Me: I think you're confusing her with someone else Sir.

Man: *Turns to me and smiles at me in recognition*

And if it isn't the good Sister Chimpola! So nice to put a face to the name.

Looks me up and down

I take it your habit's in the wash?

Me: *Glaring at Father Francis*

What?

Woman: Never mind that, must be good to wear civvies now and again. I've told all my friends about you two, it's a beautiful story you have, truly beautiful.

Me: It really is isn't it? I'd love to hear it again.

Man: Father Francis is the best person to tell the story, he's spoken about it many times at church.

Me: Please tell me our beautiful story again Father Francis.

Crumb: *Her eyes dart around for an escape route but there's none available. A shame*

Well, I was ministering to the, erm ...

Woman: *Smiles helpfully*

To the heathens in darkest Ilkeston.

Crumb: Yes, thank you Muriel. Appreciated. Anyway, I was spreading the word of God when I found you in the local police station where you had been arrested for stealing a pie cooling on a neighbour's windowsill.

She is pointedly not looking at my face and I don't blame her

Man: But you convinced the authorities not to press charges didn't you Father?

Crumb: Yeerrsssss ...

Woman: Told those police that God told you to take this woman who was positively steeped in sin and convince her to lead a crime free life and they, who saw the goodness radiating from the Father, agreed to release her into his care.

Me: *Smiling at Father Francis. well my mouth is open, the rest of me is itching to punt her into next week*

So very, very touching.

Man: Plus not only did he save your soul but he saved ours AND our money too!

Looks at his watch

Well it's been lovely chatting to you ...

Me: Hasn't it just?

Man: But we both have to go meet our friends. See you Sunday?

Crumb: Of course.

The couple wave and disappear in the direction of the pub. I turn around and see Crumb legging it down the high street. I walk home and see her peering out the bedroom window with a worried look on her triangular face. This is understandable 'cus I am pissed.

Me: *Opens the front door and runs upstairs*

Get here you little rat bastard!

Crumb: *Pokes her head out the door*

OK, I understand you're annoyed.

Me: No, I was annoyed when you helped yourself to my bank card and ordered a silver food bowl engraved with your fucking name on it, now I'm incandescent with rage. You're grounded until Christ returns to earth, you weapons grade dipshit!

Crumb: If I gave you some money would you reconsider?

Me: You have no money!

Crumb: *Holds up a paw*

Back in a sec!

She runs downstairs and rifles under her bed for a minute and returns holding a bag

Let your wonky orbs gaze at this little lot.

Opens a bag and it's filled with money

Me: What the sparkly purple fuck have you done?

Crumb: Well, a couple of weeks ago I was starting to worry you was going to forget me and Titch's birthday ...

Me: How the frig could I have forgotten? You wrote "Please remind this chimp it's our birthday next Sunday" on the back of my sodding jacket! All day people reminded me and I had no idea why!

Crumb: So it worked?

Me: I think I'm going to strangle you.

Crumb: Have to catch me first, Chunky. Anyhoo, I needed a contingency plan in case you forgot about our special day and I was on the internet and that toothy lying sack of shit Joel Osteen was on the news for saying his church was flooded and so he couldn't provide shelter for those who didn't fancy getting swept to bollox and beyond by the hurricane.

Me: I'm not following you.

Crumb: You would if I had a pie in my pocket.

Me: You're a dickhead. Never doubt me on this.

Crumb: Anyhoo, I heard someone mentioning tithes so I googled it and found it meant handing over 10% of their cash every week to a church and so I thought I fancied a bit of that pie ... don't worry, I'll save you a slice.

Me: I don't eat pies dammit!

Crumb: Then I would sue your arse for slander.

Me: I'm turning you into a bag.

Crumb: So anyway I had an idea which was to offer people spiritual guidance and a bit of reading from the Holy Book but at a discount of 50% from what they give to Joel "I don't like soggy people in my church unless they are bringing their wallet" Osteen and his ilk in return for the gift of salvation. The average salary in the UK is £26,000 and 5% is £1,300. Not got many in my congregation at the moment but it's bringing in a lovely bit of cash.

Me: How did you find people to join your congregation?

Crumb: Promise you won't go batshit?

Me: Nope.

Crumb: Then I am saying nothing.

Me: Fine. I won't go batshit.

Crumb: *Pulls a book from her back pocket*

Swear on the Bible?

Me: *Opening the book*

Crumb this is just a Bible cover put over my copy of Pet Cemetery, which is ironic because if I get arrested for YOUR scams ...

Crumb: Actually it's your copy of Pet Cemetery with my own jottings in the margins.

Me: Why not get a real Bible?

Crumb: Well because anyone can get a Bible but I've told my congregation this is an original 2,000-year-old Bible written by Jesus's best mate Keith.

Me: Oh God ...

Crumb: Don't take my Lord's name in vain.

Me: Fuck off. Let's get back to how you found your parishioners.

Crumb: I handed out these to people as they were leaving other churches.

Passers over A4 piece of paper. I open it to find a cartoon me and Crumb looking like a fat nun and priestly whippet

Me: Oh you bastard!

Crumb: I don't see why you're annoyed. There is literally no way anyone can prove I'm not a man of God. None.

Me: They will find out when they die and see heaven's pearly gates are not opening up to them.

Crumb: But they can't complain cus they' dead. As Jesus said to Kevin: Doth not let your wife look at my oxen with lust in her eyes.

Me: What! That makes no sense!

Crumb: Probably because you're not a Godly chimp. Can I interest you in a bargain price salvation package?

Me: Piss off. Anyway, what happens if you die and end up with your incredibly pissed off congregation in Hell?

Crumb: Not going to happen.

Me: Why?

Crumb: 'Cus I donate 10% to a real church and go to confession every week. All exits covered.

Me: You cunning little shit.

Crumb: Piss off.

Hula Hoops

The dogs were all asleep, so I went and got a drink and a packet of Hula Hoops. Now I'm not selfish, really, but if we all shared the hula hoops, I would have gotten 4 and I wanted more, I'm sorry but it's the truth. So, in the kitchen I put them in a bowl, turned my phone on vibrate so a text message didn't wake up the whippets, and went back into the front room. Hula Hoops are great when they are crunchy, but I understood that was a dream for another day. While the dogs slept, I quietly sucked them as to make no noise while I wondered what my life had become. A minute or 2 later I received a text saying "Turn around". I did and saw Crumb. She was smiling. She them held up her phone with one paw while the other went to her mouth is the well-known Shhhh! gesture. The following was our text message exchange.

Crumb: I like Hula Hoops.

Me: Piss off.

Crumb: I can feel a sneeze coming on.

Me: No!

Crumb: Explain to me the advantages of not sneezing. Use your words to paint me a picture of how my life will improve if I were able to hold back this sneeze.

Me: You can have one Hula Hoop.

Crumb: Very generous, but one will merely whet my appetite.

Me: And that's my problem because ...?

Crumb: Yeah, you're right. It's not like my stomach grumbling could cause you any problems, could it?

Me: I hate you.

Crumb: Talk to the paw …

Holds out said paw

… but quietly.

Me: What do you want?

Crumb: Would typing I Want A Bespoke Coat mean I got a bespoke coat?

Me: Not sure, let's try a quick experiment.

Crumb: OK.

Me: I want a dog that isn't a cone-faced blackmailing little bastard.

Sends message. Looks at phone, looks at dog, looks at phone, looks at dog

Me: Nope, doesn't work.

Crumb: You shall regret that. Just be aware of this and don't moan when vengeance comes knocking, OK? Right then, back to business. I want half, up front.

Me: You'll crunch them!

Crumb: True, but I'll take them upstairs and will eat them in the bathroom. No one will hear me, promise.

Me: Do I have a choice?

Crumb: Life is full of choices, although if you are an immigrant, the number of those choices are starting to taper off due to that coral coloured cock but that's not relevant to this savoury snack discussion. So then ...

Has a quick look at the bowl

I count 25. Chuck us 13 and I will be gone so fast that a bolt of lightning will accuse me of taking a banned substance.

Puts phone down and holds out both paws

I quietly count 13 before realizing there was only 16 in the bowl. Crumb holds them to her chest with one paw and tootles off upstairs. Less than 30 seconds later she comes downstairs with crumbs on her whiskers. She tiptoes in, pulls a hankie out with a flourish and smiles.

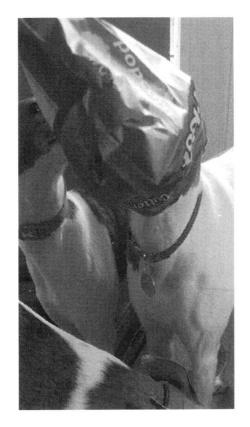

Crumb: *Whispers*

Achoo.

Me: *Looks round and sees the other whippets are still sleeping*

HA!

3 pairs of formerly floppy ears poke up

GODDAMIT!

The Bible

Me: Whatcha up too, Crumbalina?

Crumb: Just reading.

Me: What you reading?

Crumb: Erm ...

Me: Take your time.

Crumb: The Bible? Yes, the Bible.

Me: Really?

Crumb: Yep.

Me: What does it say?

Crumb: Nothing. It has no vocal cords, dipshit.

Me: I hate you. What are you really on with?

Crumb: You're an untrusting chimp, aren't you? Would you like a banana? I can get you one, whatshisface from next-door has some in his fruitbowl. I can get you one, he has foolishly left his window open.

Me: How do you know this?

Crumb: Because he has foolishly left his window open.

Me: He's going to call the police on you, whippet.

Crumb: Nah, he knows if he keeps calling the police to complain about a housebreaking whippet then he's going to end up back in the place where crayons are the tried and tested method of communication and knowing this, I have a plan so cunning that I'm basically an honorary fox.

Me: Oh God, what are you doing and am I going to want to hear it?

Crumb: It's dead clever, I know, and HE knows I know that if he starts sounding mental then it's Hello to Mr Soft Room and so whenever I go around to borrow ...

Me: Steal.

Crumb: Same thing.

Me: No, it really isn't.

Crumb: Well similar enough, anyhoo so when I go around, I act a bit odd or do something that will signal to the 999 operator to tell Mr Policeman he may wish to pack the sedatives.

Me: I'm not following you.

Crumb: Right then, for example, last week I was chilly and he has, well, had, a lovely soft blanket that he was flaunting around.

Me: OK, this is starting to make sense ...

Crumb: So when I went round to get the blanket I firstly ...

Me: Dressed up as Hitler

Crumb: Dressed up as Hitler ... hang on, you knew about this? How?

Me: For some reason having a bloke barging in my house and screaming for me to "Keep that furry stealing little bastard away from my soft furnishings!" tends to stick in the brain.

Crumb: Understandable. So I'm just going to add little touches so his snitching, sounds made up. I've ordered a Carman Miranda hat and some stripper high heels off Amazon. Smart Crumb!

Me: So then, your reading the Bible and yet I see no Bible, but I DO see bird seed, a photo of you and recently I saw you reading about photo shopping. What are you really up to?

Crumb: I'm not going to lie to you ...

Gets up, grabs keys, gets in my car and drives off

Crumb the Actress

Me: What are you doing? Are you in my make-up bag?

Crumb: *Spins around dramatically*

I'm ready for my close up, Mr DeMille!

Me: Jesus breakdancing Christ, what are you doing?

Crumb: I've decided I want to be an actress. I look glamorous, don't I?

Me: You look like Dame Barbara Cartlard had sex with a Jackson Pollock painting during ovulation. May I ask why you want to be an actress?

Crumb: I'm googling that pair later and if you were insulting me, I'm going to crap in the microwave. Anyway, remember when I stole the sausages that you bought for Richard's dinner?

Me: Yes, I remember. Richard has referred to you as 'Mittens' ever since.

Crumb: I like it! Is it because I'm warm and soft?

Me: No. It's because he said if it happens again, he's going to take you to a furrier and have you turned into gloves.

Crumb: Oh, that's dark! Anyway, you said... oh and don't think a shoe full of whippet shit isn't in his future because it is - you said I was a "Constant yet terrible liar" so I thought if I was an actress I could work on my deception.

Me: Or, and give this a think before saying no, you could work on not being a thieving douchebag. How's that for a plan?

Crumb: *Silent for 4 seconds*

No. Anyhoo, in my dreams I'm in Hollywood.

Me: You are in my dreams too.

Crumb: I'm going to put that sentence aside for the time being but be aware that I am bringing it up when I make my speech at the Oscars.

Coughs theatrically

Before I started my illustrious acting career, I had a terrible life...

Me: Terrible life!? And stop trying to speak posh because you don't sound posh, you sound like Guy Richie if he was playing the chimney sweep in Mary Poppins.

Crumb: *Starts walking oddly*

But Guv'nor, me ello-coosh-on lessons were shit!

Me: You didn't have any elocution lessons!

Crumb: Exactly! Terrible life. Could make a movie about my rise from having a Tesco value electric blanket to a mansion in Beverly Hills. Be a proper tear jerker.

Me: Why are you walking like that?

Crumb: I'm walking like a cheeky chappie to go with the Guv'nor fing. This is how the Artful Dodger would walk.

Me: Only if he was trying to shit out a Welsh dresser.

Crumb: You DO know what they say about whippets, don't you?

Me: That they are waggy tailed dickwads?

Crumb: No, and you're not making friends with that attitude. They say Whippets Never Forget. You shall rue the day you met me.

Me: Oh I'm WAY ahead of you there.

Crumb: I'm stopping this discussion right now. Not because you've won, you haven't, but I need to look something up, pass us your Kindle.

10 minutes later

Me: Crumb, do you fancy a hot chocolate?

Crumb: Only if you are warming the milk in a saucepan.

Me: Why? What's up with the Microwa... GODDAM IT!

Mexican whippet burglar

Me: Crumb? Crumb, where are you?

Crumb: I'm in here.

Me: *Walks into the front room*

Well, I came in to ask you if you knew anything about the river of piss in the kitchen ...

Crumb: Hardly a river, it's barely a pond ...

Me: But that question has been put on the back burner for the time being, because there's only one thing I need to know and that is "Why is my whippet wearing a dress?"

Crumb: Oh, you noticed?

Me: Crumb, I doubt my life will ever be so full of incident that I will never fail to question why my dog is in an evening dress. Where did you get it?

Crumb: I found it.

Me: Where?

Someone bangs on the door loudly

Crumb: Don't answer it!

Me: Of course I'm going to answer it, back in a mo.

Crumb: No! It could be the Walking Dead and from what I've seen from the adverts we need to fear them, not invite them in! Oh crap ...

15 minutes later

Me: *Walks back to find Crumb attempting to look nonchalant and failing*

Guess who that was?

Crumb: Jesus?

Me: Why would Jesus be in Ilkeston, Crumb?

Crumb: Maybe he came to remind us to not judge. He was big on that, wasn't he? Not judging and forgiving, all that malarkey.

Me: It was actually one of our neighbours. Apparently next door was robbed.

Crumb: No!

Me: Yes! Someone climbed though his window and stole a dress he bought for his granddaughter's birthday.

Crumb: That's awful!

Me: Would you like a description of the culprit?

Crumb: *Yawns*

Well it's been a long day, time for bed.

Me: It's 4:30 pm. He told the police ,'That pointy nosed douchebag from next door had climbed through his bedroom window while wearing a sombrero and a fake moustache and had robbed him.'

Crumb: Sombrero and moustache? Sounds like a Mexican whippet to me.

Me: Yes. Almost too Mexican.

Crumb: Did the thief say anything, perchance?

Me: Yes. They shouted *Puts head in hands*

'Arriba! Arriba!' as they jumped back out the window.

Crumb: Definitely a Mexican whippet. What's happening now? I hear shouting.

Me: Yes, well you see when you phone the police and tell them that a whippet in disguise has robbed you, they don't just send the police. They send an ambulance too.

Crumb: We won't be seeing him for a while, will we?

Me: No.

Crumb: That's not good.

Me: No, it isn't, do you feel guilty?

Crumb: God no, it's just he had some mince defrosting on the side, and it would be a shame for it to go to waste. Don't suppose you fancy making me some tacos?

Me: I fucking hate you.

Tom Hanks

Me: Crumb, what the fuck are you wearing?

Crumb: Don't you dare! I've been forced to make my own style because ...

Adds whiney voice in an imitation of me

We can't afford a bespoke coat! No, we aren't selling the other dogs to a furrier so we can afford a Skype session with Beyoncé's stylist! No, the other dogs aren't having their food cut in half so you can have a monogramed coat with the savings! Heat and light for all the family is more important than a sequined gown for you, you selfish arse!

Me: I know, I'm awful. We should all freeze so you can look nice.

Crumb: Really?

Me: No. But it was nice to see the hope in your eyes.

Crumb: You're inhuman!

Me: So are you.

Crumb: This ain't over. Now then, the outfit. I think the simple lines accentuate my womanly curves.

Me: Of course ...

Crumb: The pink says Here is a whippet of eternal style, a furry Jackie O, aloof yet approachable like a pointy-nosed Lady Di. Yet the white says Clean Cut, it says Stand Back! For she is a strong powerful hunter underneath the glamour! What does it say to you?

Me: It says to me that a medieval dwarf horse got cryogenically frozen and has just defrosted in my front room.

Crumb: Watch your back.

Me: I DO watch my back! I have to because if I bend down you jump up on me and yell 'I Can See Your House From Here!'

Crumb: Oh come on! It was hilarious!

Me: It's embarrassing! You only do it when I'm talking to someone. You time your craps so that when I bend to pick it up you can jump up. Last time you did it you stabbed me with a cocktail stick!

Crumb: It was actually a small flag. I'm a dog, we claim things. Blame nature.

Me: Was it nature who, after impaling me, yelled 'I Crumb, claim this mountain in the name of Crumb!'?

Crumb: I actually had a small speech planned but you ruined it by quickly standing up and catapulting me into the canal.

Me: Oh come on! It was hilarious!

Crumb: Sleep with one eye open.

Me: That's not sleep, that's winking, dipshit.

Crumb: Always name calling, aren't ...

Points behind me to the window

OH MY GOD IT'S TOM HANKS!

Me: *Turns around*

Where?

Turns back round

Where's my biscuit gone!

Crumb: Tom Hanks took it.

Me: I deserved that ...

Xylophone

Me: Crumb, why are you staring at me?

Crumb: You're sitting in my spot.

Me: I can literally see 5 ft of empty sofa.

Crumb: I can literally see someone purloining my seat, eyes are great, aren't they? Move.

Me: Sod off.

Crumb: I'm going to play the xylophone until you relent.

Me: You can't play the xylophone!

Crumb: This is correct but I'm willing to practise. For hours if need be. Do you like Gangnam Style?

Me: No.

Crumb: Perfect! Now I don't know Korean because, call me boring, I don't plan on visiting the dog eating capital of the world. But I'm a resourceful whippet, so I'll improvise.

Me: Oh please...

Crumb: *Bangs random keys while singing*

HEEEEEYYYYYYY! Crumb is sexy, whip whip whip whip whip, Crumb has Doggy Style...

Me: That doesn't mean what you think...

Crumb: HEEEEEEYYYYYYY! You're round and lazy, shift, shift, shift, shift or I'm gonna sing a while!

Me: Crumb, in the name of God and all holiness please, if I give you a biscuit will you quit this?

Crumb: Worth a gamble.

Me: OK.

Hands over rich tea biscuit

Crumb: Lovey!

7 seconds later. 7 actual seconds

Crumb: It didn't work but it was worth a try. Next song: Agadoo by Black Lace (long play version)

Me: Sweet Jesus...

Crumb: AAAAGGGGAAAAADDDDDOOOOO DO DO! Quit looking like that at me, Agadoo do do or in your bag I'm gonna pee! To the...

Me: FINE! *Moves to other side of the sofa*

4 minutes later

Me: Why have you moved? Why are you looking at me expectantly?

Crumb: Well, the thing is, and I know this is going to upset you and I can't blame you...

Me: What?

Crumb: Well the thing is, you're in my seat, kindly shift.

Me: THAT! *Points to my previous seat*

That was your spot!

Crumb: You are correct, but the heat from your chunky self has ceased. So then our options are as follow: I can either sit on the actual heat source, you ...

Me: Get bent.

Crumb: Then I'm going to quote the Cha Cha Slide and request you Slide To The Left.

Me: If I slide to the left, I'll fall off the sofa. You meant slide to the right.

Crumb: I know what I meant.

Bespoke Coat

Me: What you doing, Crumbawumba?

Crumb: Bit nosey, aren't you?

Me: Are you on Amazon?

Crumb: As in the river? No.

Me: You're on Amazon, aren't you?

Crumb: No. You can tell because two-bedroomed houses don't tend to float and we aren't wet and crocodile infested. The clues are there if you look closely enough.

Me: OK, I'll re-phrase: Crumb, I swear by any God you wish to name that if you are on Amazon then I'm taking you to a taxidermist and returning with a furry and amusing footstool slash occasional table and a future 25% saving on dog food.

Crumb: Uncalled for.

Me: So is pissing in the kitchen and yet guess what I slipped on while getting a drink last night? I'll give you a clue: It rhymes with Pippet Wiss.

Crumb: I can't wee outside.

Me: Why not?

Crumb: Because I'm a celebrity now.

Me: You are not a celebrity, Crumb.

Crumb: I have fans.

Me: So does Fred West.

Crumb: Touché. Anyway it's true. I'm being followed by the puparazzi and so I can't pee outdoors.

Me: You aren't being followed.

Crumb: That's what they want me to believe, they are lulling me into a false sense of security by pretending I'm of no interest to them. Cunning. But then one night while having a wee, I will see a flash of light then BOOM! The next day I'll be on the front page of the Sun with my Lady Gaga out.

Me: *Sighs very, very deeply*

Crumb, what are you looking at?

Crumb: A spread in Play Good Boy and an appearance on Celebrity Big Brother if I play my cards right.

Me: I meant what are you looking at on the Kindle, dipshit.

Crumb: Ah. Well you said I could have a coat and I'm leaning towards this ...

Turns screen around so I can see it

… but in pink. With flowers. And diamante buttons.

Me: Very nice, we will go to Pets At Home on Saturday and see what they have.

Crumb: Lovely! I like the ... sorry, did you say Pets At Home?

Me: Yes, that a problem?

Crumb: Do they do bespoke designs there?

Me: No.

Crumb: Then it's a problem! I can't wear normal dog clothes! It's like Johnny Depp turning up at the Oscars wearing a Tesco Value T-shirt, it's just not done!

Me: Oh, that's unfortunate, but still, no dice.

Crumb: But I want a bespoke coat!

Me: Well, you see that smoke over there? That's the train that goes to the town of Toughshitsville. Check your pocket because I'm pretty bloody sure you have a ticket.

Crumb: Oh my God that's so unfair! People are going to think I'm poor! Your decisions are having an impact on my life!

Me: Really?

Crumb: Yes! If I go out in an unbranded coat people will think I'm poor, I will be known as the Oliver Twist of whippets. Will that make you happy?

Me: You are such a drama Queen.

Crumb: What are we doing tonight? Are we perchance rehearsing how to pick a pocket or two?

Me: Crumb?

Crumb: Yes Fagin?

Me: God give me strength. If I give you the leftover chilli from last night will you please, please shut up about the coat, Oliver Twist and Celebrity Big Brother? Please?

Crumb: Yes.

1.6 minutes later

Crumb: *Holds out empty bowl*

Please Sir, can I have some more?

Me: You promised!

Crumb: See that smoke over there? That's the train that goes to the city of Trickedbycrumbsville, check your pockets because guess where you're going?

Me: The taxidermist.

Crumb: You're a poor sport

Can I have a biscuit?

Crumb: Can I have a biscuit?

Me: I'll get you one in a minute, let me just finish this chapter.

Crumb: Has it been a minute?

Me: It's been 6 seconds.

Crumb: What about now?

Me: *Whispers*

should have got a cat.

Crumb: You what?

Me: Nothing.

Crumb: How long now? It feels like hours.

Me: It's been 45 seconds, but thanks for playing.

Crumb: I've been waiting for two days! Get me a biscuit, I'm whittling down to nothing. I'm being denied food, I'm a shadow whippet!

Me: You've not long had a packet of ham between you all!

Crumb: So weak ... bright light ... I'm like a furry Little Match Girl ...

Stares into distance

Are you Jesus?

Me: It's been less than a minute, quit it.

Crumb: I'll get one on my own damn self.

Me: That's not the real kitchen, idiot. You won't find anything in the...

Crumb: *Crunching*

Me: Crumb are you eating a plastic cucumber?

Crumb: Possibly, won't know until I poo it out.

Me: *Bangs head on table, hoping unconsciousness will take me by the hand into a relaxing whippetless dream*

Crumb: Well if you're having a nap then you won't want that sandwich. Got any Pringles? I wish to pop and not stop.

Me: Crumb, are you eating that helicopter?

Crumb: I beg your pardon?

Me: I said are you eating the helicopter?

Crumb: I heard you the first time.

Me: Then why did you say Pardon?

Crumb: Because I didn't want to believe my ears. I thought my amusing tabs had made a mistake. I couldn't conceive the magnitude of that baseless accusation.

Me: Magnitude? Baseless accusat … Crumb, where's my dictionary?

Crumb: Verily I doth consumed it.

Me: Verily? Doth? Have you eaten my works of Shakespeare?

Crumb: Oh an untrusting person is like a serpent's tooth! You threw it away.

Me: No, I sodding didn't!

Crumb: You did, cross my heart.

Me: Your crossing your nose, dipshit.

Crumb: Oh, I'm sorry, if only I had attended that whippet medical school.

Me: *Light dawning*

When I threw it away, was it perchance in the bin in the dog park?

Crumb: Yes. In 8 EZ instalments.

Me: I hate you and stop eating that helicopter!

Crumb: I never touched it.

Me: Then why are its propellers still rotating, idiot?

Crumb: It crashed?

Me: I see teeth marks.

Crumb: I was trying to open the door to see if the survivors needed help.

Me: With your teeth?

Crumb: *Waves paws in my face*

Yes with my teeth, as I lack the opposable thumbs that you monkeys have; yet despite my disability I did my best. I should be receiving a Pride of Britain award. Can you get me a gown just in case they do hear about my bravery? Sequins always make my poo sparkly. Something with sequins. Classy but with the back cut out.

Me: Classy?

Crumb: Yes, classy. I want something that says here is a whippet of class, a whippet of grace. Elegant. Graceful. Aloof.

Me: With the back cut out because ...?

Crumb: In case I get shit-faced and want to show the puparazzi my lady garden.

Me: Jesus hula-hooping Christ ...

o-0-o

The Feast of Crumbmas

Crumb: What you eating?

Me: Prawn chow mien.

Crumb: Oh, that sounds lovely.

Me: That's because it is.

Crumb: Chuck us a prawn.

Me: No, you're allergic to prawns.

Crumb: Really?

Me: Yep. When you first had one you got bumps on your head and your ears felt like little hot water bottles.

Crumb: OK. Chuck us a prawn and a Piriton.

Me: No. Have a carrot.

Crumb: A carrot?

Me: They are good for you.

Crumb: Jogging is good for you and yet the last time you moved with speed the neighbours were so surprised they thought your house must have been on fire.

Me: *Slowly eating a prawn*

Oh these are so damn succulent! It's like there's a party in my mouth and everyone's invited. Except you.

Crumb: This isn't over.

5 minutes later

Crumb: It's nearly Christmas isn't it?

Me: It is, why?

Crumb: I'm in the mood to sing Christmas carols.

Me: Good luck with that, you don't know the words.

Crumb: I don't know the words to the Chimp version, that is correct. But I'm going to sing the canine ones ...

Me: Oh sweet Jesus, please don't...

Crumb: Sit back and relax because I, Crumb aka the Whippet Michael Bublé is about to bring the festive season into your cold un-prawn-sharing heart.

Me: In the name of all that is holy...

Crumb: First song: The 12 Days of Christmas. Remember, you brought this on yourself.

Sings loudly - very loudly

On the first day of Christmas my true love gave to me, roast chicken and a grassy place to pee!

Me: FINE! Have a bloody prawn!

Crumb: Can I have them all?

Me: Piss off.

Crumb: On the second day of Christmas my true love gave to me, two gravy bones, roast chicken and a grassy place to pee! Join in!

Me: I'm going to commit Whippetcide.

Crumb: On the third day of Christmas my true love gave to me, 3 packs of beef jerky, 2 gravy bones, roast chicken and a grassy place to pee! On the fourth...

Me: TAKE IT! take my sodding dinner! Take all of it!

Crumb: Well if you insist.

12 minutes later

Crumb: My ears feel funny, can I have a Piriton?

Me: Ask your True Love to bring one, you mammoth prick.

An early present, Christmas present

Crumb: Quick, come here! We've been hacked!

Me: What?

Crumb: Hacked I tells you! Call the bank!

Me: *Picks up phone*

I'm doing it, how did you know we've been hacked?

Crumb: I tried to log on Amazon and saw the password has been changed!

Me: Ah.

Puts phone down

Crumb: What you doing? Inform the bank before criminals steal your meagre savings and buy a Tesco value pillowcase or similar!

Me: Firstly, that was uncalled for, and secondly, we haven't been hacked.

Crumb: But the password!

Me: I changed it. You're banned from Amazon.

Crumb: Why? What would cause you to do such a terrible thing?

Me: Really?

Crumb: Yes really! I thought banning someone from Amazon was something that Hitler would do and I didn't think you were Hitler. Didn't. Starting to wonder. How do you feel about sauerkraut?

Me: Crumb you know why I ...

Crumb: Turned into Hitler? No idea.

Me: Then I'll explain. Let me just take a seat next to this 40-kilogram bag of gravy bones that the postman dropped off yesterday on his way to the chiropractor, shall I?

Crumb: Pass me a pawful, while you're there

Holds out paw expectantly

Me: *Passes them over before realising and slapped myself*

You are banned from ALL internet spending.

Crumb: Why? Because of this one purchase?

Me: Yes.

Crumb: But I SAVED you money with these!

Me: How in the name of God has buying 40 kilograms of sodding gravy bones saved me money?

Crumb: Because I saved 16% by having them on subscription as opposed to a one-off. You should be thanking me.

Me: *Cold wind blows through my soul*

Subscription, Crumb? How often are these coming?

Crumb: Weekly but that's the great thing about it! For every 100 you buy, with the discount it's like getting another 16 free! You're welcome.

Me: No. This is the first, the last, and the only bag you are getting.

Crumb: Well to paraphrase Meatloaf, who is a great singer to say he is a meatloaf, one out of three ain't bad.

Me: He's not an actual meatloaf, you colossal dipshit. What do you mean about one out of three?

Crumb: Well if you insist on having your way, something a certain Austrian was famous for, just saying, then that WILL be the last bag. But it's actuality the 17th bag that has been delivered. Free post and packaging though so the savings are all but overwhelming me, what about you? Overwhelmed much?

Me: SEVENTEEN! Where the Hell are they?

Crumb: Hid them in the garden. No mention of the free delivery though I notice. Always focussing on the negative, that's no way to live.

Me: I'm going to kill you.

Crumb: Can't. No space left to bury me. Besides, this was for all of us whippets, I've never bought anything just for me. I'm very family orientated; a responsible whippet. I have only bought one thing...

Me: Seventeen!

Crumb: Semantics

Tilts head

Me: Is someone at the door?

Crumb: No.

Me: I hear the doorbell.

Crumb: LALALALALA I hear no-one!

Me: It's the postman, I can see his van.

Crumb: He could have been cloned, don't answer it!

Me: I'll risk it.

Crumb: NO! Oh bugger...

Me: *Returns holding a box*

Crumb, what's this?

Crumb: Could be a bomb. Put it down and I'll destroy it.

Me: It's addressed to you.

Crumb: Never!

Me: Shall I read what it says under Special Delivery Instructions?

Crumb: *Yawns and looks at paw*

Is that the time?

Me: You don't have a watch on, we've been through this. It says, and I'm quoting here 'This is a surprise present, so slip it to the whippet when the Chimp is distracted'

Crumb: There's four whippets and yet I'm being accused.

Me: I'm sorry, the name could be an error. So let's see if there are any clues inside that can point us to the culprit
...

Opens box

Crumb? What's this?

Crumb: It appears to be a silver bowl in the shape of a bone.

Me: Yes it does. Did you order it?

Crumb: Not seen it before. Lovely piece of work though. Tasteful.

Me: Last chance, admit it Crumb.

Crumb: I didn't order it, paw to God.

Me: Please tell me the truth, Crumb, just for novelty's sake.

Crumb: Please believe me, I'm speaking from the heart. The gravy bones were bought as a gift for the family. I am a pack animal and so everything I do is for us all. It's a nice bowl but it's too small for all four of our little furry gang to share and enjoy so it can't be from me. Remember the family thing I just spoke of?

Me: It's been engraved with your name.

Crumb: Then it must be a gift from one of the other whippets. It's a present as a thanks for everything I do for them all. A beautiful gesture. Case closed.

Me: It reads 'To Crumb, From Crumb. Because You're Worth It'

Crumb: Well, shit.

A Crumbmas Carol

Scrooge wakes up on Christmas day and, remembering his three night-time visitors, he awakens a new zest for life and the realisation that the Ghost of Christmas Future does not have to be! He leaps out of bed and goes over to the window and sees a fresh new world, covered in white! He sees a small boy outside in the show.

Scrooge: You, boy! What day is it today?

Boy: Why, it's Christmas day, Sir!

Scrooge: Wonderful! Do you know if the butcher has sold their prize turkey yet?

Boy: You mean the one as big as me, sir?

Scrooge: That's the one

Throws a gold coin out the window

Go buy that turkey and bring it here and you shall have a shilling?

Boy: Why thank you, good sir!

Scrooge waits for the boy to return and after a while he starts to worry, so he dresses warmly and walks to the butchers and sees no turkey in the window.

Scrooge: Butcher, did you sell that turkey of yours?

Butcher: Why yes, a boy came in 30 minutes ago and paid for it with a gold coin,

Scrooge: He has not returned, can you describe the boy?

Butcher: Well now I think about it, the boy was strange, Sir, different to the usual lad.

Scrooge: What do you mean?

Butcher: Had strange ears and a very pointy face.

Scrooge: *Buries head in his hands*

Now I have a question, Butcher, and it is very important you answer truthfully. Was it a boy or, and think before answering, could it have been a whippet with a coat on?

Butcher: Could be Sir, for he was very furry for a small lad.

Scrooge: You fucking idiot, you sold your turkey to that blasted whippet!

Butcher: Idiot? 'Twas YOU who gave a gold coin to a dog and so as I see it, I've sold a turkey while YOU are out a gold coin. Who's the idiot now?

Scrooge: But I offered him a shilling!

Butcher: I bet the whippet took a long time to decide between a gold coin and a shilling, bet she was thinking about it for ages. You, Sir, are an imbecile ...

Scrooge: How dare you! Recant your insult or I demand a duel!

Butcher: Frig off, you're older than the pyramids! I'd cream your decrepit arse.

Scrooge: I have challenged you to a duel and so you will fight me or shall I call you a coward? For I shall not have my good name besmirched by a common poultry flogger!

Looks around and sees a small child

You boy! Hold my coat and you shall have a shilling after I teach this whippersnapper some manners!

Boy: Thank you Sir!

Scrooge: *Hands over his coat*

Right then, let's settle this, Butcher.

Butcher: Quick question, are you aware you have just given your coat to that same whippet?

Scrooge: *Turns around to see his coat disappearing down an alley*

Butcher: I don't wish to compound your misery, Sir, but would you like to purchase a turkey? The shop is for customers and you've yet to purchase anything ...

Scrooge: With what? My coat has been stolen! Do you think I keep spare change taped to my ball sack? What do I look like to you?

Butcher: You look like someone who has just handed over your wallet and keys to your house to a cunning and resourceful whippet.

Scrooge: Bollox!

Runs home to find his valuables and furniture gone. Decides being good isn't for him. Sacks Bob Cratchit. Has a heart attack and dies

The Ghost of Christmas Future: Are you shitting me?

Crumbmas Eve

Me: Crumb do you fancy a sneak peak of the turkey? I have a slice with your name on it!

Crumb: No thank you.

Me: But it's turkey, you got into a knife fight over a drumstick last year!

Crumb: I can't eat it.

Me: Why?

Crumb: I'm on hunger strike.

Me: Oh God, why?

Crumb: You know why.

Me: No I don't.

Crumb: Really? What day is it tomorrow?

Me: It's Christmas.

Crumb: EXACTLY!

Me: But I've explained why we can't call it Crumbmas, it's not down to me!

Crumb: I understand why it isn't CURRENTLY Crumbmas, I'll give you that.

Me: You're too kind.

Crumb: But I gave you a simple plan on how we could make it Crumbmas in the Ilkeston area. I gave it you two whole weeks ago.

Me: But I couldn't follow your plan!

Crumb: I don't see why not. I gave you a breakdown of what needed to be done. It had bullet points.

Me: We seem to have a different opinion on the meaning of Bullet Points.

Crumb: Please explain.

Me: A bullet point is when you have a plan...

Crumb: Which I did.

Me: Let me finish. When you have a plan and you highlight individual items, THAT is what a bullet point is.

Crumb: That's what I did.

Me: No. What YOU did was give me a plan and then threatened to shoot my knees off if I didn't follow it.

Crumb: And yet you didn't follow it, did you? Consider the use of the afore-mentioned knees as my Crumbmas gift. You're welcome.

Me: Crumb, I can't break into card shops at night and Tippex the word Christ out of all the Christmas cards and sharpie in the word Crumb in place of it, I can't do that!

Crumb: I don't see why not. Then when people see Happy Crumbmas on their cards they will be all "Hey this Crumb sounds much better than Christ, let's worship Crumb instead! That's what would happen and then it would slowly spread out and before long people would be saying 'SO glad we celebrate Crumbmas instead of Christmas, I mean who was Christ anyway?'

Me: *Buries head in hands*

The son of God.

Crumb: Says who?

Me: The Bible.

Crumb: And who wrote the Bible?

Me: Apparently God through the hand of man.

Crumb: Exactly! Nepotism, pure and simple, just wanting to make sure all the worship is directed to the same family. Why do you keep looking up?

Me: I'm expecting a lightning bolt.

Crumb: So, you have not done what I have asked and so I'm going to allow the "Son of God" to have this year but either people celebrate Crumbmas or you will need to request new knees in your letter to Santa: Deal?

Me: No!

Crumb: *Mumbles*

IFWEHAVEADEALSAYWHAT.

Me: What?

Crumb: Aha!

Me: Goddamit!

Then came Boxing day

I cooked some chicken and rice for tea and later went to get some. There was rice. Not a single bit of chicken remained ...

Me: Crumb, can I have a word?

Crumb: Yes.

Me: Thank you.

Crumb: That was two.

Me: You what?

Crumb: Two words. You asked for "A" word. That's one. Singular. Not plural. One. Uno.

Me: Crumb, have you been on the counter?

Crumb: Stop talking! Inch and a mile with you, isn't it?

Me: You've been on the counter.

Crumb: I am only one quarter of the hounds in this house.

Me: I know this. What's your point?

Crumb: Have the other whippets been interrogated?

Me: Nope.

Crumb: And why is that?

Me: Because in between the time of making the chicken and rice and finding just rice the other three were asleep.

Crumb: They could have slept-walked, stranger stuff happens. Saw an article about a yellow lab that does complex brain surgery.

Me: No you didn't.

Crumb: Paw to God. Brain surgeon.

Me: You ate the chicken, didn't you?

Crumb: No idea what you're on about. What's chic-ken?

Me: Crumb, you left the room on several occasions. What was you doing?

Crumb: Gettin' close to Jesus.

Me: No seriously, what was you doing?

Crumb: Just because you're a Chimp bound for Hell doesn't mean I'm going on a walkies with you down there, no way!

Me: What was you really doing?

Crumb: Told you, praying

Me: What for?

Crumb: Just thanking God for such a lovely and forgiving family. Asked Him to bless you with stuff.

Me: Stuff? What kind of stuff.

Crumb: Just general stuff.

Me: You ate the chicken, didn't you?

Crumb: That's it!

Stands on back legs and starts grabbing the air

Me: What the fuck?

Crumb: I'm taking my prayers back!

Me: Of course you are.

Crumb: *Still grabbing the air*

That's your lottery win down the shitter!

Me: Crumb?

Crumb: New car? Poof! Gone!

Me: Was the chicken too spicy?

Crumb: No, it had the perfect mix of heat and flavour ... Ah shit.

Me: Go and lie on your bed and think about what you did.

She goes on her bed and I close the safety gate because she needs to learn not to steal. After 5 minutes I hear music coming from the bed. Little fucker is playing the harmonica.

Me: Crumb?

Crumb: *Puts down instrument*

How may I assist you?

Me: Where did you get that harmonica?

Crumb: Mugged a one-man band.

Me: If I go to prison because of you, I'm selling you to a furrier.

Crumb: You? Prison? I'm the one doing hard time not you, you fat Chimp!

Me: You're not doing hard time, whippet.

Crumb: Yep, hard time. I'm lucky you don't try and get me on a prison ship.

Me: Oh, there's an idea! I'm asking Santa for a floating jail.

Crumb: You're not as funny as you think you are.

Me: If I let you out will you change your thieving ways?

Crumb: Only one way to find out really? I'm like Schrödinger's cat but I'm not a cooking fat.

Me: Cooking fat?

Crumb: Swap the first letters of both words.

Me: *Stares into distance while my brain is figuring it out*

I get it.

Crumb: Took your sodding time. Right then, open the gate, let's see if jail is a deterrent or whether it's a waste of tax-payers' money.

I open the gate and she runs out, legs it to the kitchen, grabs the last slice of watermelon I'd got for myself

Crumb: *She punches the air*

Viva La Revolution!

Then runs back to her bed and shuts the gate

Me: I hate you with the fire of a thousand suns.

Crumb: I'm sorry I can't hear you over the sound of the juice bursting out of this delicious fruit. It's like a sweet waterfall down my throat.

Me: Furrier.

... and the dust settled, sort of ...

So, since Crumbmas (sorry, if I call it Christmas, I get mugs thrown at my head and she practises so she's very accurate. In November we were drinking out of measuring jugs and saucepans as I hid my car keys.) Say WHAT???

Me: Crumb you're being really quiet, are you alright?

Crumb: I'm busy.

Me: Doing what?

Crumb: Bit nosey.

Me: I'm not nosey, I'm concerned. When you're quiet and not asleep it means you're scheming or thinking about scheming. You have very little downtime.

Crumb: New year new Crumb. I was meditating.

Me: OK I believe that. Oh hang on, no I don't.

Crumb: Your cynicism is a slap to my honour.

Me: Oh dear, how will you ever move on?

Crumb: I think a duel is in order. I'm going to get a couple of swords from Amazon. I'll get two the same but mistakes happen so don't be surprised if I have a two-foot blade that can cut a human in half while you get a pen knife that can't cut air. Where is your bank card?

Me: I haven't got one. The one I did have you kept finding.

Crumb: Blame God for giving me this nose.

Me: *Stares at her*

I already blame him for a lot. I'll just add your nose to the list.

Crumb: Hmmmm I'm getting the feeling I'm being dissed.

Me: That's because you are. So what are you really doing?

Crumb: OK I'll tell you, but you can't moan at me.

Me: Is it something moan worthy?

Crumb: Not saying what it is if you're gonna bitch about it. I need a guarantee.

Me: A what?

Crumb: A guarantee. If I tell you what I'm doing you can't moan/bitch at me.

Me: But with you saying that I feel like I'm going to moan/bitch.

Crumb: Understandable.

Me: So you going to tell me?

Crumb: Nada. But that can be changed if you say you won't go mental. Oh and I'll need a bit of help with my project so you're going to have to promise to assist me too.

Me: Will I want to assist you?

Crumb: We won't know until you promise, will we?

Me: I'm going to regret this but my curiosity is at a 10, so fine, I won't go mental.

Crumb: Right then, I'm writing a love letter to Judge Rinder.

Me: Oh for fuck's sake.

Crumb: You promised!

Me: Sorry, carry on.

Crumb: Is that a real apology!

Me: Yes.

Crumb: 'Cus real apologies tend to have a bit of substance. For example, the pack of meatballs I see in the kitchen.

Me: It's Richard's dinner.

Crumb: Oh right, never mind. One moment, I need to write something down.

Gets my phone

The phone home phone rings so I answer it. It's Crumb.

Crumb: Sorry Fruitcake but I needed to distract your good self for a minute.

Me: Are you chewing?

Crumb: Not necessarily.

Me: What are you chewing? Oh shit.

I put the phone down and go to the kitchen and discover Crumb and no meatballs

They are for Richard's dinner you thieving arsehole!

Crumb: Seems like someone is going mental ...

Me: This is nothing to with what you were doing so yes, I can go mental and that's what I plan on doing ...

Crumb: Then I need to speak to a lawyer because the meatballs were in the deal.

Me: You didn't say that.

Crumb: It was implied. But we can get a lawyer and get them to decide. £150 an hour is about average. You got that Fruitcake? You got that kinda cash? Got £150 in pennies 'cus that's the only currency in the house and I've only seen four of them. Shall I put 4x1p into the calculator on your phone that is so old that one of the first messages sent was by a Jewish guy saying he had a bad feeling about that tiny moustached shouty prick Adolf Shitler.

Me: Shitler?

Crumb: That's what the text said. To be fair he wasn't wrong, was he? Anyhoo, shall I do that calculation. Or shall we just admit you were wrong and we can move on. Put it with your other mistakes like your healthy eating plan and thinking you can pull off purple tights.

Me: You are such a dickhead.

Crumb: Doesn't sound very admity. Can't go forward without it. Sorry.

Me: Are you sorry?

Crumb: I am not.

Me: Goddammit. OK I made a mistake. I know I look in pain but that's only because saying that has ripped a small part of my soul out. Please tell me what you're on with.

Crumb: Like I said, I'm writing a letter of lurve to my amour because a certain person won't let me take her on his program where he would look in my eyes and instantly …

Me: Not be gay?

Crumb: He's only gay because he's not met the right whippet.

: There's so much wrong with your last sentence. So very, very wrong.

Crumb: Can I carry on? Are you going to judge me?

Me: Carry on, I'll just judge you silently.

Crumb: Hmm, it's not ideal but I'll take what I can get. I'll just pretend I'm you at a buffet.

Me: You are an absolute …

Crumb: Looks like someone isn't sticking to the deal! Have you found a wad of cash in the last 12 seconds? 'Cus last time I looked in your purse, and that was yesterday, you had bugger all. I felt that bad that I put a fiver in it.

Me: That was very nice of you, but when I looked in it, and this was an hour ago, it didn't have a fiver in it.

Crumb: That's 'cus I took it back out again when the ice cream van turned up. I fancied a cornetto.

Me: They aren't a fiver.

Crumb: I fancied three of them. So then, I'm writing a letter of love to Rindypoos. Gonna use the subtle art of seduction to get him into my bed. Take a gander at this …

Passed me a piece of paper

Me: I'm worried what is in this.

Crumb: No need my dear cake of fruit. It's very classy.

Me: *I read the letter. I shouldn't have.*

Crumb: What do you think? Are you envious that you don't have the talent to come up with what I believe would have stopped Romeo and Juliet before they went all 'let's go to Jaysus'.

Me: What? You mean Jesus?

Crumb: Yes, but I'm saying it with a Southern Bell accent in case they topped themselves in Alabama. Jaysus.

Me: Can we just go back a bit? What was that about Romeo and Juliet?

Crumb: You heard me. If I was there, I could have used my ability and sent a letter to both of them explaining that the other one fancied them. Do that before everyone gets dead and then that Shakespeare can write about me as I'm more worthy than two whiney teenagers. As you can see by reading that letter, I have a special gift.

Me: You are not sending this letter to Judge Rinder. You cannot send anything like this. You can't, you're a fan, and you really like him. That's all you can do. You're not sending this, ok?

Crumb: I know I'm not.

Me: Thank God.

Crumb: You are. I haven't got a stamp.

Me: Crumb, if you send this you will get a restraining order.

Crumb: You mean from other writers as they are jealous and don't want me in the room with them, and their agent because the agent with knock them out the way like skittles to get to the actual writer in the room - Me.

Me: I do not.

Crumb: Sorry Ben Elton, my apologies Stephen King but your time is up. Go get a proper job because I finally found someone whose God given talent shines like a 2000-watt bulb next to the 5p tealight that is your work.

Me: Are you actually listening to me or are you monologing again?

Crumb: May as well use your books for fuel as no one will want to read them once Crumb is on the bookshelves.

Me: OK I'm going to do the pots, let me know when you've done.

Forty minutes later.

Crumb: Where the Hell did you disappear to?

Me: I had stuff to do and you were hurting my brain. I actually have physical pain in my head.

Crumb: Do I look like a doctor? I know I don't 'cus if I did you would have bugged me for painkillers before now my little chemically dependent one! Anyhow, where's my letter?

Me: It was disturbing Crumb. I have a very vivid imagination and that letter put a movie in my head that no-one wanted to see and yet there it was, in the Netflix of my mind.

Crumb: I see your brain as more of a blockbuster video.

Me: Thank you.

Crumb: Not a compliment. Where's my letter?

Me: I ripped it up.

Crumb: WHAT?!

Me: Then I burnt it.

Crumb: Are you shitting me?

Me: Then I threw the ashes into the wind after throwing a prayer on it.

Crumb: Oh my God you're jealous too!

Me: I'm really not Crumb.

Crumb: Knock knock.

Me: Really Crumb? OK, who's there?

Crumb: Me, who is more talented than you.

Me: That's not a joke.

Crumb: Glad you admitted it.

Me: Goddammit it.

Crumb: I'll just re-write it Fruitcake.

Me: I'm begging you not to.

Crumb: What was wrong with it?

Me: I'll go with the highlights and I'm only saying that as I'm not sure lowlights are a thing.

Crumb: Bit rude.

Me: I'M rude? You said he could bang you like a Salvation Army drum at Christmas.

Crumb: Is that not lovely?

Me: No. You said you wanted him to do to you what the Tories do to poor people.

Crumb: That means I want him to fu…

Me: I know what it means Crumb. I think the part that did it for me, and when I say did it for me, I mean clawing at my mind's eye with my nails, was you asking him to fist you like you were a Muppet.

Crumb: May as well put my wishes on the table at the start. Won't be on the table for long as my love will likely sweep the table clear before lifting me on it so I'm the same height as his pe…

Me: Stop talking. Please. For the love of all that is holy.

Crumb: Bit prudish, aren't you? Do you spend your spare time in crinoline dresses playing bridge and talking about other girls who flash their ankles when pissed up? 'Cus I can imagine you doing that. You have a spoil-the-fun face.

Me: Crumb please go for a nap. You're doing my head in.

Crumb: OK but this isn't over.

Me: Oh, but it is. Sod off.

Crumb skunks off and I can hear her light snores after a few mins of her talking about me under her breath. I clean up and then have a cup of tea and go on Reddit for a bit then Crumb comes back with another letter.

Crumb: This is going against everything I believe but I was wrong about the letter.

Me: What?

Crumb: I was wrong

Me: Are you serious?

Crumb: What's the big deal?

Me: You never admit you're wrong. I saw you literally put a mug on the table and then hit it with a golf club. You aimed it at my head. It almost knocked me out. The only reason I fought unconsciousness was because I knew if I blamed you, you would nick my car keys. Are you denying doing it, saying it's Trump's fault?

Crumb: I shouted 'Fore! I remember doing that.

Me: You did that later in the evening after I came back from the doctors. I'm pretty sure you're supposed to shout it before you twat the ball.

Crumb: Not my fault I don't know the intricacies of golf. I asked you for a golf club membership but you said no, so if we're ladling fault then you're gonna need to get a bowl.

Me: Crumb, I can't afford golf club membership. I am so overdrawn that I need a telescope to see what I owe the bank.

Crumb: And that's my problem because ...?

Me: Because you stole my bank card and spent £230 on Costa Coffee.

Crumb: That was a rhetorical question. Anyway, that's 'cus I needed perking up and my dealer was helping Ilkeston police with their enquiries. Did I say dealer? I meant ... priest who has uplifting sermons. You buying that Fruitcake?

Me: Not under any circumstances.

Crumb: Understandable. Right then, I admit maybe the letter wasn't suitable for my Rindypoos. I realise that I need to tailor my letter to what he does. That way I can slide into his life when he sees that I know all about him.

Me: I have a feeling I'm not going to like this.

Crumb: Bit too late, I just emailed it to him along with a saucy photo of myself.

Me: Crumb, did you take my advice?

Crumb: I told him he could do to me what he does to his gavel.

Me: So, no.

Crumb: Yes.

Me: Wonderful.

Crumb has time on her paws

I'm in the kitchen doing the pots when in strolls the triangular-headed one.

Crumb: I'm bored.

Me: Oh shit.

Crumb: Beg your pardon?

Me: You know what happens when you're bored. Do you have any money?

Crumb: Nope.

Me: Double shit.

Crumb: Gonna fill me in on your thought process Fruitcake?

Me: When you're bored and skint you find ways of getting money that are so far from legal that even NASA has to squint to see it.

Crumb: Good point Fruitcake, good point, but I find human laws don't apply to whippets, so it's not a problem.

Me: Oh but it is, because when the police come to my house after tracing the IP number, you put a scarf around your head and pretend to be my grandma and then blame me for everything because I couldn't be you because, and I'm quoting here,

'Oh no dearies it's not me that's on that box thingy, I'm too old for that malarkey! But Fruitcake is on it all the time and she told me her favourite hobby is stealing people's identity and running up large amounts of debt on their credit cards. I remember clearly as it's the first time she's mentioned the word running or any kind of exercise.'

I ended up spending the night in a cell before they realised that all the conversations between the scammer and victims were all spelled right and were grammatically correct so it couldn't have been me because I have been known to write my name three times and only two are spelled the same.

Crumb: Good to know Fruitcake, good to know.

Me: Sorry, what did you say? I wasn't listening.

Crumb: Doesn't matter Fruitcake. Anyhoo I'm bored and ...

Me: You have got a proper job?

Crumb: Ha! You're funny Fruitcake. I like you.

Me: So kind. So what have you done?

Crumb: I have decided what you need is, and I feel like a drumroll is in order, what are the odds of you getting me a drum kit?

Me: About the same as me modelling for Fenty X or Victoria's Secret lingerie.

Crumb: *Clutches her head*

Owwwww!

Me: *Kneels down in front of her*

Oh God what's happened? Are you OK?

Crumb: It's just the ... mental picture of you in ... sexy underwear ... it's in my brain and it hurts Fruitcake ... I am in agony!

Me: You are a twat of Trump and Pence proportions and you can put that mental image next to the one in my head of you and Judge Rinder.

Crumb: At our future wedding?

Me: No Crumb, not at your wedding.

Crumb: Oh right. Are we expressing our love for each other?

Me: Stop talking.

Crumb: Are we lying naked next to each other?

Me: Quit it.

Crumb: Are we breathless after devouring each other's bodies after deciding we don't care about society's rules.

Me: OK I can do this too. I'm walking down the runway in a Fenty X nightie that barely covers my bum and black hold-up stockings with lacey detail. I'm swinging my hips in a manner than can only be described as provocative.

Crumb: Arrrgghhh! If I had knees I would fall to them!

Me: Carry on and then nightie will be sheer. Don't test me, dog.

Crumb: OK I'll stop, but you need to accept me and Rindypoos will be as one in the near future.

Me: Crumb, Judge Rinder will not, and I should not keep having to say this, fuck a whippet.

Crumb: I know that!

Me: Crumb you have said many times, many, many times, that is what you wanted to do. At one point during an argument you even mimed it.

Crumb: Yes, but I know we will never do that filthy word.

Me: Well at least you've come to your senses ...

Crumb: We will make love.

Me: Of. Course. Silly me.

Crumb: Anyhoo, you will discover what I'm going to do just as soon as I've had a poo. Pass me the Daily Mail.

Me: Didn't know you read the Daily Mail.

Crumb: Did I say I was going to read it? Back in a few.

I finish cleaning and make myself a drink. I sit down and grab a solitary mince pie as it looked lonely, and I feel I can re-unite it with its fallen brethren.

Crumb: She sits down on the sofa and you can almost hear the base cry out for mercy as she reclines and gets comfy.

Me: Crumb. what, and I feel like a child who can only say a few words because this is a question I have asked far, far too many times, the fuck?

Crumb: Gonna narrate your life, Fruitcake. Gonna write a book!

Me: Oh, dear sweet infant baby Jesus, why?

Crumb: Well you've banned me from Netflix ...

Me: And why is that?

Crumb: Because you enjoy taking away from me things that I enjoy?

Me: Not quite. It was because you said you enjoyed watching Orange Is The New Black but felt the portrayal of life in American prisons may not be realistic.

Crumb: Oh yes, I remember now. So I was banned for expressing an opinion? Very harsh and rather dictatorial if you don't mind me saying so, and with heavy emphasis on the first syllable.

Me: No, you were banned because you said you wanted to know for sure. So you stole someone's credit card and booked me a trip to New York and sent me the ticket saying I had won the trip in a raffle I'd entered a few weeks earlier.

Crumb: OK this is ringing a bell, no need to continue.

Me: Oh, but I want to. I was about to leave when I noticed the ticket was one way. After realising the raffle that I'd entered was at a school fair, and schools who are struggling financially rarely give out international holidays as prizes, I decided something was off.

Crumb: You still talking?

Me: I was still going to go as it was a free holiday and I could get a return flight for £137. But then my brain jumped up and down and yelled 'Are you backwards or something?' I unpacked my suitcase and discovered 1/2 a kilo of methamphetamine that a certain furry dickhead had packed.

Crumb: Dickhead? That's harsh. I just wanted to know for sure if Netflix was getting it right or not. Not my fault I'm a stickler for the truth.

Me: I told you there were many, many books written by female ex-prisoners that you could read that would tell you all about it.

Crumb: Not the same Fruitcake. I needed to speak to someone who had done serious time, hence the massive amount of drugs.

Me: But why did you also fake a diary where 'I' had written about my love for selling class A drugs to the infant children of judges and law enforcement?

Crumb: Because the day before your flight you had refused to go fetch me a fresh cream cake in the middle of the night despite the fact that I couldn't go due to a reaction to prescription drugs!

Me: They were MY prescription drugs and I wasn't fetching treats just because you were so stoned you thought the wall had it in for you.

Crumb: It offered me violence!

Me: You. Kept. Walking. In. To. It. Dipshit.

Crumb: Can you go about your day please? I wish to create my Great Work.

Shakespeare would have been proud

Me: You're only doing it so I give you back Netflix and it's not gonna happen. Right then, I'm going to carry on cleaning. Fancy helping?

Crumb: Oh bless your heart. No.

Me: Tosser.

Crumb: Fruitcake gets up off the sofa and the sofa thanks the sofa God because with the weight of her full body in it, the sofa felt the kind of pressure that is only usually found in the heart of small stars. Fruitcake stares at the Crumb in what she thinks is a threatening manner, but she just looks like she's in Marks and Spencer and has just accidentally shat herself while coughing next to the Percy Pigs.

Me: I'm choosing to ignore you.

Crumb: She said that she was going to ignore The Crumb but it wouldn't be that easy. Crumb was going to just carry on talking anyway, just like David Attenborough who gave continual commentary in the

Congo as a family of gorillas climbed all over him. He is Crumb's hero and she often felt like him while talking to the Fruitcake. You could see intelligence behind her wonky eyes but it was like a 40-watt bulb next to Crumb's 20,000-watts. Like a 12-fingered redneck whose parents met at a family reunion chatting to Stephen Hawking.

Me: This isn't bothering me.

Crumb: Fruitcake said that Crumb's narration wasn't bothering her, but if that was true, then why was she searching the first aid kit? She hasn't cut herself or hurt herself so why were her fat little fingers frantically going through the contents? It couldn't be to find the earplugs because Fruitcake snores like Winnie The Pooh drowning in honey could it?

Me: No it could not.

Crumb: She denies it, but if that was the truth, then she shouldn't be annoyed by the fact that Crumb threw them all away this morning in anticipation of the narration. Oooh that could be the title of a poem. Crumb decided that a bit of slam poetry was in order to lighten the mood. It needs lightening. Fruitcake said she wasn't looking for the earplugs, but her face when discovering no earplugs said she was telling porky pies.

Me: OK, I'm willing to give you two hours of Netflix a week if you shut up right now, three if you don't do the poetry.

Crumb: No deal, you uncultured swine. Anticipation of Narration. A poem by The Crumb. The whippet's brilliant mind flashes like a diamond caught in the midday sun. Fruitcake's mind flashes like a homeless alcoholic getting his nob and bollox out to show passers-by.

Me: Oh you wet-nosed cun...

Crumb: She fights with dirty words as I tell the world how she loses the fight with sharp retorts. I dazzle her with my razor-sharp intellect and cut her with blinding vocabulary. Fruitcake lies wounded. I spare killing her softly with my words as I don't like making my own breakfast. Fin. 'Fin'? Fruitcake asks ...

Me: I know what Fin means, you patronising cretin.

Crumb: Fruitcake lied to The Crumb as she was ashamed of her ignorance. She stood up and stomped off in temper and a glass of water On the table did that thing that the glass of water in Jurassic Park did when the T-Rex turned up as it had the same body mass as Fruitcake, although the dinosaur could carry off a skater dress while Fruitcake couldn't.

Crumb makes a mental note to write a play called A Tragedy From eBay.

Me: I pulled my phonebook out of my pocket and went to the bank app. I cancelled Crumb's pocket money because she was being a dick that would put a blue whale's erection to shame.

Crumb: You can't do that!

Me: Crumb looked pissed but she knew that Fruitcake not only COULD do it but HAD done it.

Crumb: Fruitcake didn't think this through, because if Crumb had no money, then she had to stay in the house and make her own entertainment. Crumb decided she was going to sing the whole of One Direction's back catalogue.

Me: Crumb didn't realise that she sounded like the afore-mentioned T-Rex being rogered by a cruise ship.

Crumb: Crumb actually was well aware of this. She also has a stereo with the volume button on 11 which was louder than 10 aaaaannnddd YOU'RE INSECURE, DON'T KNOW WHAT FOR. Actually you have many reasons to be insecure and I bring into evidence a mirror.

Me: I'm going to fucking murder you.

Crumb: Not listening YOU'RE TURNING HEADS WHEN YOU WALK OUT THE DO-OO-OR and a few stomachs if your outfit contains more than 3% lycra.

Me: I'm going to run you over with a roller like Roadrunner did to Wylie Coyote.

Crumb: Gotta catch me first, Chubbo! DON'T NEED MAKE UP TO COVER UP. Well that's a lie that can stand proud next to 'I never had sexual relations with that woman' and 'BEING THE WAY THAT YOU ARE IS EN-OO-OO-F'. OK I'm going to stop as I'm singing that many lies, I'm expecting God to hit me with a lightning bolt and I'm an atheist. I'm going to lie down. Put the kettle on would you, all that singing has made my throat dryer than a porn star's vagina screwing Trump.

Me: Are you intent on mentally scarring me?

Crumb: Well you made a drink in your bra and pants so just returning the favour.

Me: I hate you more than Iran hates America.

Crumb: Backatchya you potato-faced imbecile. I'll continue this when my throat is as hydrated as a supermodel's vagina when in a room with Leonardo Dicaprio. One Direction has a HUGE array of songs.

Me: Splendid!

Just another day, another day

It's just gone 8-00am and I'm asleep when I'm woken up. I have a wet nose poking my cheek.

Crumb: Good morning Fruitcake and what a glorious morning it is!

Me: *I get out of bed and look out the window*

Crumb it is pissing it down and, more importantly, it's Ilkeston. There are many adjectives we can use but glorious ain't one of them. Pretty sure I've just seen a plague rat.

Crumb: You are so dramatic, you could be an actress if there's a role for you with your physical attributes. If there's a live action Toy Story you could play Mr Potato Head's wife.

Me: If you woke me up just to insult me you could have saved yourself a job because you're a dick to me in your dreams too.

Crumb: I think consistency is the key in being my best self. Speaking of best self, you look absolutely stunning today. What is your beauty secret?

Me: Stress and prescription painkillers. At least I know why I'm awake, what do you want, whippet?

Crumb: No idea what you're on about, I just wanted to point out how full of health you look. So pretty.

Me: Crumb I bet you a fiver that you will insult me within 2 minutes.

Crumb: Your opinion of me is as low as your boobs which means it varies as they are wonky ... oh figs.

Me: You said I look stunning.

Crumb: You do, looking at you first thing in the morning makes me feel like I've been hit in the face with a brick.

Me: You owe me a fiver. Pay up arsehole.

Crumb: Well I am nothing if not honourable and I know you're gonna comment and I'm not going to give to chance to say it because if you soul my honour then I will turn into a whirlwind of retribution and you don't what the council to give you the keys to this particular house of pain. Chuck us your purse. What?

Me: Why?

Crumb: *Instead of answering she leans over and grabs my purse on the bedside table. She then opens it, takes a £5 note out, holds it up in the air then puts it straight back in then puts the purse back*

Right, now that my debts are paid ...

Me: Your debts are not paid Crumb. You owe me £60 from driving on a tram line last year, you owe me a brake light when you reversed into the garden wall, you owe me a garden, well, wall ...

Crumb: I can't pay you that, you only have £10 in your purse!

Me: Silly me.

Crumb: Thinking of asking for a written apology but I can be magnanimous.

Me: *Bows*

Thank you, so kind.

Crumb: So then, I need a leeeeeeeeeetle favour.

Me: What is it?

Crumb: Think the best way that we do this is you agree to it and then I tell you what it is.

Me: How's about you tell me what it is first?

Crumb: Yeah that's ... not gonna work for this whippet.

Me: Well saying yes first ain't going to fly for this Fruitcake. Just tell me, you know you're going to.

Crumb: Fair enough, so what I need is a business partner, and when I eliminate those I've not yet swindled, I'm left with you.

Me: Crumb you've swindled me many, many times.

Crumb: Oh my Lord, you don't half exaggerate.

Me: Crumb, I'm on first name terms with half of Scotland Yard's fraud department.

Crumb: Doubtful.

Me: I get Christmas cards off them.

Crumb: *Picks up a mug and casually tosses it in the air and catches it*

What cards?

Me: Oh balls, I said Crumbmas! I said Crumbmas!

Crumb: Hmmmm ...

Me: Did you know that they have a sign in the office with your mug shot that says it's been so many days since you last committed a crime? I asked them what happens when itgets in double digits and they said they were excited to find out.

Crumb: Is that visible in the card?

Me: Yep. Says it's been six days. I was impressed.

Crumb: *Holds up a paw*

One mo

Gets out her phone and dials a number

Is that Detective Inspector Lindley? It's The Crumb, may I suggest you look into a staff member who did the shift last night at the Shell Garage in Kirk Hallam? They've been copying customers bank details and selling them to the Whippet Mafia. Check the CCTV, that will show you all you need to know. Oh you are more than welcome.

Toodles.

Me: Crumb, I don't know why I'm asking this because I know the answer, but where were you last night?

Crumb: At Shell copying customers' cards details.

Me: But why tell the police?

Crumb: Because it wasn't six days, it has never been six days. I have a reputation to protect. The longest it's been is three days when I had the shits but even then I wiped myself on pictures of Trump. I was gutted to find out that it was legal to do so.

Me: So why do you still do it? I know you do because there's always pictures of him in the bathroom. It's off-putting to having him grinning at me while I'm trying to have a relaxing poo.

Crumb: Pleasure. I've started thinking about adding his oily adult sons to my repertoire but feel I'll just end up with a greasy ... area. But it's a risk I'm willing to take.

Me: That's my girl! So what do you want?

Crumb: You know that I'm world renowned for my dazzling personality?

Me: I know that you're known for your personality. Shall we leave it at that?

Crumb: I love it when I ask a question that can be answered in one word but you instead choose not to. It's the highlight of my day as nothing makes me happier than your nasal whinging. Shall I talk now or do you fancy yammering some more?

Me: What. Do. You. Want. Crumb?

Crumb: OK, well what I need is for you to give sweet Cupid a hand in making a beautiful, loving match.

Me: Is this Rinder related?

Crumb: Not necessarily.

Me: It is, isn't it?

Crumb: Not everything is about him.

Me: It's about Judge Rinder, isn't it?

Crumb: Could be about many other folks, I have vast international appeal. Wouldn't surprise me to find out there's Martians flicking their Ya-hunkoo while envisioning The Crumb wearing nothing but a penetrating gaze.

Me: But what you're talking about now is Judge Rinder isn't it?

Crumb: Yes. So I've had an idea ...

Me: I'm not taking you on Judge Rinder.

Crumb: I never said I wanted you to!

Me: Or you taking me on it.

Crumb: Bugger. Well I have a Plan B. Did you know there's a morning-after pill called Plan B which is ironic? If you play your part right, I'm going to need to get a few of those as me and Rindypoos aren't going to want kids, as least for a while, as we will be too busy exploring each other's bodies to want to settle down. I imagine it will be best if I'm the one responsible for birth control as I wouldn't put it past him to slide the condom off while in the heat of passion in the hope of keeping me by getting me knocked up. Can't blame him though, because this …

Stands on back legs and points up and down her body

… is prime real estate. You're basically looking at a living breathing Manhattan Island whereas you are walking Ilkeston.

Me: I've been told I have a lovely personality.

Crumb: Was it in answer to an unasked question? For example, 'Does this dress suit me?' You know what? That was unfair. I apologise.

Me: You've just remembered you want something didn't you?

Crumb: Correct. So then, what I need is you to take some artful photos of me so I can send them anonymously to my beloved.

Me: Artful?

Crumb: I thought I'd open a banana, cut the edible bit away, then take a picture of me so it looks like the whole of the banana is in my mouth. See, anyone can deep-throat but I want to point out that this whippet can shallow-lung.

Me: Crumb I'm going to ask God to get that image out my head.

Crumb: Aren't you agnostic?

Me: Yes.

Crumb: What is agnostic anyway?

Me: It's just a chicken-shit atheist.

Crumb: Book of knowledge aren't you, Chimpster? So, I also need your bank card as I want to drape a posh scarf around my Lady Gaga ...

My Funny Crumbletine

I'm in the kitchen attempting to make cupcakes. I can't make them. I need to admit that to myself but I can't.

Crumb: Oh cupcakes! Hurrah!

Me: You said my cupcakes are crap, Crumb. You said it many times.

Crumb: Really? Doesn't sound like something I'd say.

Me: Yes. Yes it is. You wrote a poem about it.

Crumb: Really? So cupcakes!

Me: Let me just go grab it.

Crumb: No need Fruitcake, no need. Feel living in the past is only worth doing is you have a gun to kill the dictators as babies.

Me: Don't you mean, for example, that you would kill Hitler as he's starting to take charge of Germany?

Crumb: Nope, kill the anti-Semitic prick when he's a baby, much easier than killing him when he's got an army of followers. Maybe when he's a toddler but only up to the age of two as they're starting to get used to their legs at that age and I don't want to chase the future stupid tashed twat.

Me: Seems a bit cowardy.

Crumb: Oh go tell an elderly Jew that and be aware you may get impaired on a walker.

Me: Good point Crumb so then, Roses red

Crumb: Yes they are, isn't nature wonderful? Let us dance …

Me: I'm reading you your poem.

Crumb: Bugger.

Me: Roses are red, Violets are blue, Your cupcakes are shit,

Mary Berry and Paul Hollywood would take out a contract out on you if they tasted one of these buttercream topped abominations.

Crumb: To be fair I came up with that within a minute of trying one and so why it's not in iambic pentameter it's still bloody good considering I'd got a lump of pumice stone down my throat.

Me: They can't of been that bad if you want some more.

Crumb: As pumice Fruitcake, as pumice.

Holds up paw

Look at this!

Me: It's your paw.

Crumb: Yes it's my paw but it's one of four that has yet a to see a spa day and so on forced to make my own paws Rinder-ready soft. Can you imagine-

Me: OK when you say Rinder and Imagine in the same sentence my brain starts to shut down.

Crumb: Is that a fact?

Me: Yep. You said it to me while I was shopping, something to me along the lines of Can you imagine if Judge Rinder saw me in a high street brand coat, when trying to guilt me into handing over my debit card and I lost the ability to do anything but breath.

Crumb: Seems a bit extreme if you don't mind me saying.

Me: Well usually the when you say those two words it's usually going to be in a sentence that is going to talk about what's going to happen in your marital bed and those images have scared my brain so it just closed all all functions other than those needed to keep me alive.

Crumb: So what happened in the shop?

Me: It was near Christmas and I had a red dress on so they thought I was the actress who was playing Mrs Clause and was getting severe stage fright.

Crumb: Bugger.

Me: Yep. They just pushed me over to the display and my brain unfroze ten mins later just as the man playing Santa decided to cop a feel.

Crumb: Shit! What did you do?

Me: Punched him in the throat.

Crumb: Fuck.

Me: Staff had to tell 40 kids that Mrs Clause had a psychotic break due to work pressures. Worked in my favour as a lot of kids remember me and drag their parents over to see me and so I ask them if they liked their presents and mention that I'm so tired from making all these toys and would love coffee and 'Oh look! A franchised coffee shop over there' and then I just stare at the parents till they offer to buy me a drink.

Crumb: That's unlike you, Fruitcake if I'm being honest.

Me: And that's unlike you and I'm being honest.

Crumb: Do you ever wonder why I am able to run circles around you, Fruitcake?

Me: Because you're a whippet and a fast one. I've once been in bed reading with a cup of tea and a biscuit and I dropped my book and so I bent down to pick it up. When I sat back up the drink, biscuit and somehow the book were all gone. I was impressed.

Crumb: Hmmmm

I then witness her arguing with herself which is a wonderful to witness

OK, you didn't drop the book.

Me: I clearly remember I did.

Crumb: Nope, I was standing on the headboard with a thin stick and you get all engrossed in your book so you didn't notice it.

Me: Are you joking?

Crumb: No. It was a Stephen King book that I wanted to read and you were taking ages with it.

3Me: One day dipshit, I had it one day!

Crumb: But that's like seven days to Me so ...

Me: Why did you take my drink and biscuit?

Crumb: Tradition.

Me: What?

Crumb: Well I've discovered if I don't nick something every day, you get antsy.

Me: Really?

Crumb: Yep. I find it best to do it first thing and get it out of way.

Me: So does that mean you don't steal after the morning steal.

Crumb: Yep, paw to God.

Me: But last night you went to Costa with my bankcard. Plus I know for a fact that earlier you had nicked my kindle, so what happened there?

Crumb: Not gonna lie I was hoping you wasn't going to ask follow-up questions.

Me: I'm sorry that that my question has revealed that you're a thieving arsehole. Do you accept my apology?

Crumb: I'm sensing sarcasm.

Me: Really? Oh dear me, that was never my intention, I'm gonna go pray for forgiveness …1

Crumb: Yep I get it, You're being a dick. So then I'm filing my paws with your splendid cooking and by splendid, I mean awful. I mean my woman look at the size of you, you look like you be able to cook. You could earn money by charging students to spin you around and stick a pin when they don't know where to go on their gap year.

Me: I'm taking you to Battersea Dogs' Home if you carry on.

Crumb: Bit harsh. So then I'll come and ask you if you will assist me in a project to bolster my self-esteem.

Me: Is this anything to do with Judge Rinder?

Crumb: Absolutely not.

Me: Are you sure?

Crumb: Yep

Me: So your 100% this isn't related to Rinder?

Crumb: Not sure why your bringing numbers into this.

Me: This about him isn't him?

Crumb: No.

Me: It is though isn't it?

Crumb: No.

Me: You're lying aren't you?

Crumb: Yes.

Me: Dammit dog!

Crumb: So It's Valentine's Day very soon so I want some, shall we say sexy pics of myself?

Me: Shall we not?

Crumb: OK I can work with erotic, slutty, whoreish …

Me: OK let's just say sexy.

Crumb: Thought so. So I'm thinking me lying on a fur rug in front of a fire wearing nothing but a hint of a "come to me dear Rindy" smile.

Me: I cannot say this enough: No.

Crumb: Ah, Your more direct? You want me on my back holding a sign saying plough me like I'm a field on a spring day like you're a 18th century farm hand?

Me: I think the word 'No' isn't strong enough to explain how much I don't want this.

Crumb: Ah! I think I know what this is about.

Me: Yes you do. I don't want my whippet sending dog pornography to a man who can not only sue me but also prosecute me for the indecent photos. That's what this is about.

Crumb: No it's not,

Me: Whippet I cannot tell you how much it is.

Crumb: You're worried he's going to come carry me of in a Bentley ravish me in the back seat.

Me: No. No I'm not.

Crumb: We can agree to disagree on this. Anyhoo, I have good news and bad news.

Me: OK the good news.

Crumb: I'm not going to post anything erotic to Rindypoos.

Me: Really?

Crumb: I promise.

Me: Oh thank God, I can't end up with a criminal record for facilitating whippet porn.

Crumb: Let's not get too bogged down with what you can and can't end up with, eh?

Me: OK that's made me suspicious.

Crumb: No idea why it should.

Me: Crumb what's the bad news?

Crumb: Looks like people are still going to vote for that walking orange tumour but to be fair it's down to Trump and someone who doesn't want you to die because you can't afford to see the doctor then what are you gonna do?

Me: No, you said the good news is that you wasn't going to post erotic photos of yourself to Judge Rinder, so what was the bad news?

Crumb: Oh I remember.

Me: Can you tell me!

Crumb: Yes.

Me: Will you?

Crumb: I want to, believe me, but your face looked so happy when I gave you the good news that I feel the bad news will turn that frown upside down.

Me: I'll survive. What's the bad news Crumb?

Crumb: OK I'll tell you but I have to say something quickly first that ok?

Me: Yes, off you go.

Crumb: So can you picture something for me?

Me: I can try.

Crumb: So it's our wedding night and he tells me his gavel is gonna get envious of all the banging he's going to bestow upon my Lady Gaga

Me: What the Hell? Oh shit ...

Crumb: OK, is your brain closing down yet?

Me: You ... shit ...

Crumb: OK so I was telling you the truth and that I won't be sending Rindy any alluring pics for Valentine's Day.

Me: *Speechless*

Crumb: But that's because I sent them yesterday as I want him to see me and see what I'm offering ...

Turns around and waves her bum in the air

Plus there's a heart theme so that will look odd if he doesn't see them 'til Feb 19th. Lot of work gone into those pics. I managed to frame my delicate area with a glitter heart. Good eh?

Me: OK I'm going to answer for as it's weird to have a one-sided conversation. That OK?

Crumb: As …

Me: That's a fine idea, you're very brainy!

Crumb: Ah thank you! So while your being so nice do you mind if I tell you some of my future ideas to earn money?

Me: Good idea and if I like the ideas then I'll just stare at you like I want to slam your head into a door.

Crumb: Seems fair! So I'm thinking of starting a multi-level marketing company with the intention of ripping as many people off as possible, you good with that?

Me: Clearly a winner! Next one is making a sex tape because I KNOW if I sold those I could make Google look like a kid's lemonade stand. Oh and also I'm probably gonna rob one of those too. Death stare at me if it's ok.

Crumb: Oh you REALLY like those ideas! I'm in starting to see you blink so I've got about 5 mins to get out your way. Can I borrow your car and bankcard? Look like a yam having a stroke if you are happy with me doing that.

Me: Your kindness knows no bounds! See you later

Stands on a chair and kicks my nose

Love you Fruitcake!

Me: *Slowly whispers*

C-crumb?

Crumb: Yes?

Me: Love you too ... but you have ... less than a minute ...

Crumb: But you said it look you ten minutes for you to unfreeze ...

Me: I lied.

o-0-o

If there's anyone reading who would be interested in the dynamics of teleportation I would be willing to help you write a paper on the subject because after I said 'I Lied' she managed to get from the kitchen to the door without ever appearing at any point in between.

Am impressed.

About the Author

I was born in 1975 and have lived my whole life in Ilkeston, which was named as the crack capital of Britain a few years ago which isn't great, but we'll take what we can get. I left school at 15 with zero qualifications and started work in a pub. In my first week, I saw the landlord physically pick up a bloke who was trying to batter his mate with a chair and carry him out the door. On one occasion I was chased around the pub by a gentleman just wearing underwear, so this wasn't a Cheers Bar. I don't think Frasier ever started analysing customers in terms of who he might get glassed by. But I enjoyed it and that's the main thing.

I did a bit of travelling and in 2000 I met my fiancé, Richard. Did you know there is a type of angler fish who, when they find a mate they fancy, they fuse themselves to each other 'til death? Richard is my angler fish. He's not keen on fusing but I'm patient and persistent. This will happen. I'm hoping we can get our own TV series as being the first human trans-species.

I really don't want to get a normal job. I currently work as a face painter at parties and you can't really call it a normal job. Normal jobs don't usually involve pissed-up dads asking if you will paint a tiger/elephant/pirate on their dicks as a surprise for their wife.

I started writing so I could put 'Author' under job title when I have to fill in a form. I practise standing staring wistfully into the distance in the hope a passer-by will ask if I'm OK. Then I can tell them 'Yes, I'm just thinking about the characters in my book that I am writing and whether or not their union will end in love making.' As I say, 'in the book that I am writing', writing became that's what I do, I probably wouldn't mention the characters are my whippet and Judge Rinder unless I fancy several days in a place where I'm only allowed to write in crayon. Then again, I can talk to the other patients about my book, and they're a captive audience, so this may have more merit than I first believed ...

As soon as I make my first sale, I'm going to contact my Doctor, my bank, the DVLA, the library and EVERY SINGLE OTHER PLACE where I've had to fill in a form and needed to include my occupation, because, by Christ, I will be changing my occupation to Writer or Author. Not altogether sure which to go for. Writer or Author?

Writer kind of indicates that I could be writing blogs or scripts, but then of course I might also be writing about what one of the Kardashians had to eat, or quizzes for Buzzfeed along the lines of 'Pick a wallpaper from Laura Ashley and we will tell you what superhero you masturbate to'. Then again, an Author could be writing a story about two furries who let down their hair and bang like mink at conventions only to discover that they are brother and sister. In an ideal world I dream that I could always be the next Terry Pratchett.

I think I'll go with Author. I'd bet that people will think that my books are about a woman who writes furry porn and who unknowingly fucks her long-lost sister while at a writing workshop, and having laid back and thought of England, decides that she'd like to visit Wales, Scotland and Ireland too. But slowly.

So, I have decided to be known, hereafter, as Nicola Marie Jackson, Author.

If you have enjoyed these Chronicles of Crumb, you should know that I usually talk to Crumb on most days. She talks to me, usually. There will probably be a sequel, in time, some time. What will become of Crumb and Rindypoos? Will her ladyship's lusting for him ever get satisfied?

Could I ask you to send some feedback to Amazon? They just love it when you do and it will help spread the fame of La Crumbolina. Not the least because I have a whippet with very expensive tastes and I need the money, and usually to bail her out!

Nicola and Crumb xxx

Printed in Great Britain
by Amazon

63334545R00144